HIDDEN POWERS

ALSO BY JEANNINE ATKINS

Finding Wonders: Three Girls Who Changed Science
Grasping Mysteries: Girls Who Loved Math

HIDDEN POWERS

Lise Meitner's Call to Science

JEANNINE ATKINS

ATHENEUM BOOKS FOR YOUNG READERS

New York   London   Toronto   Sydney   New Delhi

$\mathcal{A}$
atheneum

ATHENEUM BOOKS FOR YOUNG READERS

An imprint of Simon & Schuster Children's Publishing Division

1230 Avenue of the Americas, New York, New York 10020

For information about special discounts for bulk purchases, please contact Simon & Schuster Special Sales at 1-866-506-1949 or business@simonandschuster.com.

The Simon & Schuster Speakers Bureau can bring authors to your live event. For more information or to book an event, contact the Simon & Schuster Speakers Bureau at 1-866-248-3049 or visit our website at www.simonspeakers.com.

Interior design by Jacquelynne Hudson

The text for this book was set in Arno Pro.

Manufactured in the United States of America

1221 FFG • First Edition

2   4   6   8   10   9   7   5   3   1

Library of Congress Cataloging-in-Publication Data

Names: Atkins, Jeannine, 1953– author.

Title: Hidden powers : Lise Meitner's call to science / Jeannine Atkins.

Description: First edition. | New York : Atheneum Books for Young Readers, [2022] | Includes bibliographical references. | Audience: Ages 10 and up. | Summary: A biographical novel in verse about Lise Meitner, an Austrian Jew and physics professor in Nazi Germany who escaped to Sweden and whose work led to the discovery of nuclear fission. Includes author's note and timeline.

Identifiers: LCCN 2021010848 | ISBN 9781665902502 (hardcover) | ISBN 9781665902526 (ebook)

Subjects: LCSH: Meitner, Lise, 1878-1968--Juvenile fiction. | CYAC: Novels in verse. | Meitner, Lise, 1878-1968—Fiction. | Physicists—Fiction. | Women scientists—Fiction. | LCGFT: Novels in verse. | Biographical fiction.

Classification: LCC PZ7.5.A85 Hi 2022 | DDC [Fic]—dc23

LC record available at https://lccn.loc.gov/2021010848

With love to

Emily Laird Dresser and Scott Dresser

The Longest Day

Smoke sprawls past the train.
Passengers lift knitting needles or open books,
but don't count stitches or turn pages.
At last the locomotive screeches to a stop
at a station. Peddlers pass broth
and sausages through windows.
Uniformed men with guns pull people
off the train, crying, pleading.

Lise tries to keep her hands steady
as an officer studies traveling papers
printed with lies meant to help her escape.
A Jewish scientist isn't safe in Germany,
but she was forbidden to leave.
Lise silently counts seconds, aches to taste hope.

Lessons in Astonishment

Rain taps the windows.
The three sisters make believe the parlor
is a dangerous, beautiful forest.
The oldest girl pulls a shawl over her head
like a red riding hood. The second-to-oldest
fills a real basket with imaginary gingerbread.
The third doesn't want to be a grandmother,
a hunter, or a wolf. There should be more choices.

A clock chimes. Their father shuts his book.
The two older girls don't want to get wet,
but Lise races their father down the stairs to the street.
He opens an umbrella. She steps out of its shelter.
Horses pull carriages through puddles.
Her father cheerfully greets a policeman: *Guten Tag!*

As the rain stops, Lise skids down a grassy slope
by the river, reaches for wild violets.
Her father, whom she calls Vati, takes her hand,
says, *Nein. Those aren't ours.*
She looks up as red, yellow, green, blue,
and purple stripes soar and bend over the river.
She asks, *How is a rainbow made?*

Mist left in the air after rain
splits sunshine into its colors, like a prism, Vati says.
The rounded backs of raindrops bend the beams.

As Lise raises her arms, he laughs
and says, *No one can touch a rainbow.*
She keeps her hands high
with the hope of being the first.

Embroidery

Soon after Lise's baby brother learns to stand,
a new baby comes who needs to be carried.
Lise escapes to her grandmother's quiet bedroom,
which smells of candles and perfume
from a bottle with a small red cap.

She holds a round frame that pinches cloth
with barely visible spaces in the weave.
Omi, her grandmother, tells her to count the stitches
she crosses to blend shades of red for a rose.

As she threads a needle, Omi talks
about how, long ago, her family came here
to Vienna, where she grew up among
other Jewish refugees, married, raised children,
and every day thanks the Lord for blessings.

When Lise asks about where she came from,
Omi squints as if smoke stings her eyes.
Liebe, darling, it's best to leave troubles behind.
She tucks away thread, needle, and scissors
shaped like a bird with the blades as a beak.
We'll finish later, but not tomorrow.
The sky will fall if you sew on the Sabbath.

Omi lights two candles.
She covers her eyes and says a blessing
before the darkening sky brings in a new holy day.

Lise pricks a needle through the cloth,
pulls the thread down and up. She waits,
looks out the window, and keeps stitching.
An experiment. The sky stays
where it belongs. Or does it?
Darkness and light don't keep perfectly still.

The Tall Door

Lise and Gusti cut out paper crowns.
They pretend to be princesses or royal cats
while their older sister starts school.
The next year Gusti leaves home with Gisela.
In the evenings, Gusti teaches Lise the alphabet.
The twenty-six letters can be made into more words
than you know how to count, at least yet.

When it's Lise's turn to start first grade,
each sister holds one of her hands as she skips.
They stop in front of a beautiful wide door.
Lise understands she's meant to enter alone.
Her collar and sleeves seem terribly tight.
You taught me the alphabet, she says.
Can't you tell me what else you learn?

We can't teach you everything! Gusti exclaims,
then whispers, *Remember you have brave sisters.*

Everything is what Lise wants to know.
She pushes open the door.

Vocabulary

Desks must be lined up perfectly straight,
the teacher says. Chairs pulled in just so far.
Lise learns the proper way to grip
a pencil, hold a ruler steady. She lines up letters,
then links words into more meaning.
She sits among girls with nearly paper-pale faces,
dark hair pulled back into braids.
All wear skirts and carefully hidden petticoats.

Lise learns that the word "daydream"
means thoughts belonging to her alone.
The teacher says: *Don't.*
She learns the word "shy" is close to "goodness"
but feels like a stone in her chest.
Words that slide easily at home
stick on her tongue in school.

Wrong Answers

After their mother checks for lights-out, Gusti whispers,
Would you rather see the future or be famous?

I want to see what will happen, Lise says.

Would you rather be invisible or able to fly?

Fly.

Would you rather be pretty or smart?

The sisters have a rule that they must choose
just one answer, but Lise understands
this question is a trap. Gusti wants to know
if she'd rather be like their smart oldest sister
or pretty like her. Lise says, *Nobody*
when she really means herself.

The Edges of Wonder

Lise memorizes poems and practices
multiplication tables. She wonders
how many times you can multiply something,
then multiply that again and again.
Division, too, can go on forever.
What happens if you try to split the invisible?

The teacher slaps a yardstick on Lise's desk.
Pay attention!
Lise pulls back her hands, sits up straighter.
Being almost invisible doesn't keep someone safe.

Without Boundaries

Lise likes school more when science is taught.
She flattens flowers inside books,
then pastes them on paper, labeling the parts.
She learns a little about storms
and how electricity moves through metals.
She learns that the word "theory" means an idea
that comes from looking closely and asking questions.

Lise's teacher twists a strip of paper,
attaches the ends into a loop. She introduces
a Möbius strip, a path of paper with just one side.
What seemed impossible is not.
Joy ripples through Lise, but her body stays still.
She feels part of the world
held within a memory in the making.

Two Candles

Lise is twelve, and both older sisters have stopped school,
when their grandmother becomes too ill to leave
her bed. She looks small under the covers.
As Omi sleeps, Lise studies the two candles
she used to light on Friday nights.
Omi told her that one flame honors the present moment,
the other memory. Lise asks her mother,
Do prayers work if you're not religious?

We've always been and always will be Jewish,
but your father and I look ahead more than back.
Let others stand to worship in synagogues
on Saturdays or kneel in churches on Sundays.
We do our best simply to care for all people.

But do prayers work if you're not sure they're heard?
Mutti looks her in the eye—a day Lise will remember.
She says, *Prayers are as much hope and love as words.*

The Street

Mutti covers the parlor mirror with black cloth.
Guests sit on cushions or stools,
blowing their noses in handkerchiefs,
saying nice things about Omi. The table
is covered with half-emptied cups and plates.
The edges of sliced challah bread turn hard.

Mutti asks Lise to mind her little brothers and sisters.
When the eighth and youngest child gets restless,
Lise counts on her fingers to show Walter
there are just two more days of company.
He whispers, *I don't want Omi to be dead.*
But can I ever play again?

Lise takes him outside to the street
where children chase a rubber ball.
They scramble and shout until
three tall boys swagger toward them.
One spits and says, *No Jews allowed here!*
He kicks the ball in front of horses
pulling a carriage. The ball pops.
The driver jumps down from his seat
and chases the bullies.

Walter tightens his face to keep from crying.
He looks up at their window
and asks, *Does everybody die?*

Someday. The truth keeps Lise's feet steady
as boys shout. A horse whinnies and stamps.
Walter, this is everyone's street,
Lise says. *You can play here.*

14

Saved

Lise winds toy trains, spins tops,
organizes games of cards and hide-and-seek.
She helps her youngest brother set up tiny towns
with old boxes, spools bare of thread, pencils,
and the red cap from the empty perfume bottle.
They line up their father's leather-bound books
as a bridge. Walter asks, *Why are these books so big?*

Vati says laws are short
but have long stories behind them.

Lise passes along their grandmother's
old tales about rivers, rain, and floods.
Walter opens the roof of a toy ark.
He plucks out two wooden ducks,
donkeys, elephants, lambs, and lions
shrunk to the same size. There are two people:
Noah and his wife, who must have a name.

Lise taps her fingers like rain. She says,
The whole world flooded, but Noah called
animals to the ark where they'd be safe.

Walter wiggles the animals, gives them a voice.
They're crying. They miss their old home.

They find a new one, Lise says.
Finally the storm stopped. A rainbow came.

But all the good people were saved, Walter says.

No. Lise tells him the truth.
She hopes someone on that ark asked,
Why just us? Why not everyone?

Broken Promise

Lise's teacher holds up a chart showing
the stacked squares of the periodic table.
Inside each square stands one symbol for elements
that she says make up all the parts of the world.
Every person is made of elements. Every tree.
Some elements are ordinary and often around.
Others are rare. Some haven't yet been found.

Elements seem like the alphabet of the world!
They're as essential as letters—half-forgotten
by readers used to skimming through sentences,
but necessary to make each word.
Lise's mind brims with questions,
but before she can pose them,
the teacher puts down the chart with symbols
arranged as if in a tiered jewelry box.
She doesn't say, *You'll learn more next year,*
as boys might be told in the school across the street.
They will keep on with classes, while
those for girls end when they turn fourteen.

Lise looks out the window at a world dividing in two.
What's called "pride" in boys

is called "bragging" in girls.
What's called "humble" in boys
can make a girl disappear.

Fourteen

Boys run past Lise and other hungry girls,
shout and swerve into friends on the street.
Lise doesn't want to walk in a straight line
heading home to pin, button, buckle,
tend to her five little brothers and sisters.

Sometimes she wishes she were a boy,
though it's not her own self she wants to lose.
How many people can she be and leave behind?
Years ago she stopped pretending
she was a princess, a cat, or all-knowing,
her hands hovering over small wooden villages,
inviting Noah's animals onto strawberry farms.

Now she walks without a paper crown, warns
her little brothers and sisters, *Be quiet, be careful.*
Heading to the park, Lise tells them
to look before crossing the street
and to seek the police if they ever get lost.
She lets them pluck violets growing in the grass,
watches out for bees and boys who wave sticks.

The Knife

Lise bends over a book while Gusti combs
lotion through her hair to loosen its crinkles.
Gusti's hair falls downward rather than coils.
Her blouses stay tucked into her skirts.
She pushes in pins, trying to stab Lise's hair
into obedience. She pokes her back. *Sit up straight.*

I'm reading. Lise bends deeper over
a French grammar book.
She's taking classes to train to be a tutor.

You should come with Gisela and me to parties,
Gusti says. *You need to meet boys.*

Ouch! Lise twists away from Gusti's pins.
I never know what to say to them.

Just say anything. But not about math.

Lise attends some dances. She also volunteers
in a hospital with her older sisters, making up beds
or bringing patients pitchers of water.
She doesn't like chatting with them.
Instead she finds work in a kitchen, cutting

vegetables for soup to feed the hungry.
She wants to be good, and more.
Still, all the chunks of potatoes and turnips
look like a pale path without an end.

The Birthday Present

The periodic table takes up two pages
in the book Vati gives Lise when she turns sixteen.
Hydrogen and helium grace
the top of the grid, as if floating.
In the middle, metals like copper, silver, and gold shine.
To the right are softer metals often used
to make things, like tin, aluminum, and lead.
Around them a cloud of symbols
stand for elements as important and unseen
as the places where stories begin.

Science becomes a need, like hunger.
One world whispers questions.
Another tells her to turn her back.

The Café

Newspapers from around Europe are draped
from a wooden rack in a café.
For the price of two cups of mocha,
Gusti studies arts and fashion articles
while Lise reads *Le Figaro* to polish the French
she tutors to daydreaming girls.
Like Lise, many are seventeen.
Most seem to be waiting for another life
they call marriage. Lise is waiting, too, though
for something she can't name. Each year without schooling
marks how far she is from where she wants to be.

When Lise folds the newspaper, her sister talks
about the opera they'll attend tonight
and her dream of playing piano on a stage.
Gusti turns her head, frowns at men
at a nearby table laughing over glasses of beer.
She whispers, *They're discussing who's prettier,*
using a nasty name for Jewish girls.

Ignore them. Lise tucks her head.

Of course. That's what we've been taught.
Gusti stands, smiles, and walks through cigar smoke

past the table where the speaker sits.
She swings an arm so his coffee cup spills in his lap.
He howls. His companions snicker.

Pardon me, Gusti says, turning to take back
her seat with grace, as if before a piano.

One

Lise pries a story she needs from news reports
about a scientist ten years older than her.
In Poland, where colleges are also closed to women,
Manya Sklodowska worked as a governess to help
pay tuition for her older sister at the University of Paris.
In turn, that sister supported the younger one
while she earned a degree in physics.
Now French enough to call herself Marie,
she worked with, then married, Pierre Curie.
They discovered two elements.
Marie named radioactivity, a force
that can burn a way through paper, cloth, or skin.

Knowing one woman did such work
is like switching on a lamp. The darkness is gone.

What Can Change

Lise opens the book Vati gave her
and shows Walter her favorite two pages.
The symbols for elements stand in rows
straight as bookshelves full of possibilities.
*Each element has a story of what it is
and what it might become,* she says.
*Marie and Pierre Curie discovered two new ones.
You can't see polonium or radium,
but their rays can burn.* Lise dips her pen to write
the symbol for radium in an empty block.

You're not supposed to write in books!
Walter's eyes widen.

When people find out more, we need new words.
Lise runs a fingertip below the rows of boxes.
The periodic table can change shape and size.

Why do we need more elements? Walter asks.

*We can't yet know the use of such discoveries.
But we have to keep looking.
Long ago alchemists thought an element
like lead could be changed into gold.*

Then scientists said no, elements can't change.
Now radioactivity shows that elements can transform,
giving glimpses into elements not yet named.
If what's known about the natural world can change,
so can the places where girls should or shouldn't go.
Hope is found and lost, slips in, then away.

Laws

After the supper dishes are cleared, everyone sings
while Gusti plays the piano. Then the youngest head to bed.
Others scatter to corners or chairs with books.
Lise checks one sister's knitting, points out a missed stitch.
She says, *It's hard to spot a mistake until you've knitted*
far enough to see a break in the pattern.

Her sister cries and runs to their mother.
Lise helps another sister who keeps forgetting
the answer to eight times seven.
She slams shut her book, says, *I hate math.*
You're lucky you're done with school.

We're not lucky, Lise says.

I'd like to study more too, Gisela says.
At the hospital, I listen in to doctors.
I could do more useful work than changing sheets.

Vati puts down his newspaper. *Men claim*
that more than nine years of school
harms girls' health. It's nonsense.
I read that colleges opened for women
in England, France, America, and Switzerland.

I wish colleges would open here, Lise exclaims.

Maybe they will. Laws aren't bricks.
They can bend, Vati says. *I'll help all*
my daughters go to college if you get that chance.
It won't be easy. It was lonely being one
of the first Jewish students in my law school.
But somebody has to go first to make things fair.

The Chance

At last justice—don't call it luck—
takes the side of women in Austria.
Shortly before the new century starts,
colleges will admit those who pass the entrance exam
given to boys after four years of preparatory school.
Lise buys and borrows books,
reads while ironing her little sisters' dresses.
She works her way through books on botany,
zoology, mineralogy, psychology, religion, Latin,
German literature and history, mathematics,
and the briskly changing field of physics.

Lise reads in the parlor while Gusti practices
Brahms pieces she'll perform in fancy parlors.
The counting at the piano, the patterns of pauses,
build on the old to find a new way to wonder.
Science, too, is built on practice and attention
until something small widens or rises beyond facts.

Light Within Stones

Lise's dress swings over her ankles as she passes
a butcher's shop, fruit and vegetable peddlers.
She and her sisters no longer hold hands,
but Gisela and Gusti walk beside her, humming,
on their way to classes in medicine or music.

Lise strides past pillars and through the wide doors
of the University of Vienna. In the corridors,
men swerve or sigh to let her know she's in their way,
though at five feet tall she's smaller than most.
Portraits only of men hang on the walls,
as if to suggest that while women students
may now enter, they can't leave a lasting mark.
Passing a few other young women, Lise recognizes
the armor of shyness, the glint of determination.

Lise is the only woman in a hall of one hundred men
who study physics in 1901. She takes notes
on the ways sound, heat, and light merge
like three instruments into one piece of music.
Her favorite professor dances between
three blackboards, exploring matter and energy.
Questions and answers are more circle than line.

Laboratories are in old buildings with buckling floors.
Walls with wormholes shake in high winds.
Lise measures radiation on patched-together equipment.
She analyzes samples of radium Marie and Pierre Curie
gave to the university in thanks for Austria's gift
to them of pitchblende, dark ore they crushed
and filtered to find new elements.
Lise looks close, determines when to believe
her own eyes and when to follow the math
that lies beneath, like light within a stone.

Intermission

Lise and Gusti buy tickets for cheap balcony seats,
lean toward musicians who lend their breath
to trumpets, softly stamp fingers over flutes,
scissor elbows by violins, or skim hands
over a piano, blending, widening
until strangers around them feel like family.

During intermission Gusti sometimes says,
One day I'll perform here. Tonight she talks
about a young man who's studying to be a lawyer.
With Justinian I found the music I sought.
Lights flicker. Musicians settle back in their seats
to play Beethoven, a crash, cry, and long goodbye.

One Note

After the cherry orchards across the Danube River
bloom, Gusti marries. The ceremony is simple.
Justinian's family is much like theirs: Jewish
but more devoted to music, art, and books than ritual.
The next year Gusti gives birth to a boy.
The patience she brought to the piano is given
to drying infant tears and changing tiny nightgowns.

Lise misses the echo of her sister's footsteps
and ambition, but she walks to the university alone.
In lecture halls, she steps over the sprawled legs
of young men who always believed
they had a right to sit here. Lise takes exquisite notes.
She stays up late reading to make up for the years
she waited for a college to let her in. But even
as she forges forward, she never wants to leave
the laboratories where wind whistles through thin walls.

Lise completes almost two years' worth of work in one.
Just after cherry orchards again turn pink with blooms,
Lise visits Gusti, who makes her steps small enough
to match her little boy's. Robert sprawls under
the piano to feel the floor shake as his mother

taps out a song. She sings: *One yellow duck, two, three yellow ducks! Quack-quack-quack!*

At the end of the song, Gusti strikes one key. A deep note echoes. Her voice sounds small. *It's the same music from a parlor as on a stage.*

The Calling

After Lise earns a college degree, she starts graduate school.
Now she spends more time in laboratories than lecture halls.
Most textbooks are outdated, so she searches
scientific journals, orchestrates information
about the latest discoveries in radioactivity.
These invisible rays suggest how atoms
shape the particular characteristics of elements.

Every answer Lise uncovers raises more questions.
After earning a PhD, she continues her research.
Men give her tips on how to use a hammer and saw
to build worktables. Everyone shares ideas
for putting together wires and glass and metal pieces
to make equipment. Lise loses the tight sleeves
of shyness when talking about work she loves.
Still, she aims to look meek for now.
She'd rather be called shy than a show-off,
but being cautious is exhausting.
She wants to matter. Is that selfish?

Lise's third paper on radiation
is published in a prestigious science journal,
signed: *Dr. L. Meitner.* Her name in print

lets her imagine being worthy enough
to learn while working beside
the first woman to win a Nobel Prize in science.
Lise writes a letter to Dr. Marie Curie.

Sorry

When Lise learns there's no place
for her in the Paris laboratory,
she tells herself she'll find other chances.
But when Gusti visits with her boy,
Lise's throat is sore as she says, *Maybe I'm not good enough.*

No one works harder than you! Gusti's voice
rings with loyalty. *There could be a hundred
bad reasons why you didn't get that job.
Could Madame Curie be anti-Semitic?*

*No. I read she's faced name-calling herself,
I suppose because of her hair.*
Lise runs a hand through her own determined curls.
Polish, Jewish, it's all the same to bigots.

Her nephew looks up from toys on the floor.
He asks, *What's a bigot?*

A coward who can't see truly, Lise replies.

Robert picks up the wooden ark,
spills ducks, horses, and birds over the carpet.

Lise reaches over Noah, picks up the woman
who bore and raised three children
and likely tended the animals, too. She survived
a flood. At least her name should be known.

Eight Ways

Lise helps her mother cook for a gathering
of relatives after a sister's wedding.
An aunt says, *You'll be next, Lise,*
as if life were a straight road and she's in line
for bouquets or babies.

The conversation turns to applesauce and socks.
Lise sits on the floor with her nephew,
coaching Robert in addition as he stacks blocks.
Gusti asks, *Don't you want a child of your own?*

Lise bristles at the question many ask,
if not always in words.
She's already rocked a lot of babies,
taught enough toddlers how to butter toast.
She says, *No child could be as dear as Robert.*

If your mother and I wanted all our children
to be alike, we might have stopped
at two instead of eight, Vati says.
We don't expect all to have the same calling.

The Motion of Light

Lise marvels at a lecture given by a visiting physicist.
Max Planck speaks of charting the spectra of heat
moving from red to orange to blue-white,
finding not a smooth rise but one that's staggered.
He suggests radiation moves not in waves,
as most thought, but pulses in small separate particles
he calls quanta, distinctive as the ticks of a clock.
Mystery is as much a part of math and science as fact.

After Max Planck leaves the podium,
Lise calls up her courage to speak with him.
He looks about her father's age and is formally dressed,
but squirms boyishly while discussing his formula,
which explains some qualities of light but muddles others.
It's unsettling that the atomic world doesn't seem
to follow the laws of the world where we stand.

Lise wonders what it would be like
to discover something you don't entirely love.
After Dr. Planck returns home,
she mails him copies of her published papers.
He writes back, noting she might find work
at the university in Berlin, Germany. Another country.

The Path

Lise says goodbye to her family by the door
of the apartment that smells of coffee,
floor wax, and leather-bound books. Mutti says,
I hate to think of my girl alone in a foreign city.

Berlin is as civilized as Vienna, but with more science.
We share a language and much else.
Staying between the same walls can be dangerous too.
Lise turns to her father, who sees where she stands.
He promises to send money while she gets settled.
Gusti says, *I could never leave where we grew up.*

Omi did. Lise still doesn't know what happened
to make her grandmother flee her homeland.
It's just for a year or so.

Gusti's little boy says, *Where are you going again?*

Germany. Lise hugs Robert, who asks,
Where Hansel and Gretel got lost in the woods?

They found their way back home.
Lise swings Robert in a circle

until he cries, *Don't break me, Tante Lise!*

Never! She puts him down.
He slips something into her hand.
She makes out the shape
of a wooden beak and a tail that curves up.
He says, *Mama said you can take the duck*
so you won't be lonely. The ducks are my favorite.
They aren't scared. They can swim.

The Exception

Lise sets her yellow gloves beside her on the train seat.
She looks out the window at the Danube River,
cornfields, and views of the snow-capped Alps.
By the time the train steams into Germany,
women swap magazines. Children bounce on the seats.

In Berlin, flat bridges span a river that doesn't ripple much.
A statue of a winged goddess stands on a stone arch,
raising a wreath in one hand, a weapon in the other.
Lise finds the University of Berlin. She remembers
holding the hands of her sisters on her first day of school.
She still calls herself shy, but she just traveled to a new country.

Max Planck, the distinguished director of sciences,
greets her politely but informs her
that women in Germany can't enroll in university classes.
Besides, you already have a PhD.

I want to learn more.
Lise is afraid she misunderstood his letter.

Nature designed women to be hausfraus and mothers.

Max's steel-rimmed glasses balance on his thin nose.
But I don't want to stand in anyone's way.
I've accepted a few young ladies as students.
They can't get credit, but I found their work quite fine.

A Friend

Max invites Lise to attend his lectures
and weekly colloquiums in the physics building.
There, people from various departments, cities,
and even countries listen to scientists speak.
Lise is the only woman among men who glance
at her, then away, like birds sweeping toward a branch,
then flying off, as if deeming it unworthy of landing.
But after one Wednesday lecture, while
Lise pours coffee and hands around china cups,
Otto Hahn introduces himself.
He says, *I've read some of your papers.*

And I've admired yours on discovering mesothorium.

Which I thought was a new radioactive element. Ach,
I was told perhaps a mix of thorium and stupidity,
Otto replies, though the discovery was sound
enough for him to be named a professor.
I'm afraid the chemists here aren't keen
on my radioactivity experiments. And to go further,
I need someone clever not just with test tubes,
but a physicist who knows her way
around machines that measure heat and light.

Otto calls over the head of the Chemistry Institute.
He asks if Lise might join him in the laboratory.

Dr. Meitner, your credentials are impressive,
Emil Fischer says. *But we don't allow ladies
in the chemistry building. I'm afraid
their hair may prove a fire hazard
near the open flames of Bunsen burners.*

Otto raises thick eyebrows over his blue eyes.
Surely we scientists can find a solution.

Sidewalks and Stairs

Narrow basement windows face the street.
Lise happily sorts wires, tubes, tin scraps, and papers.
Otto carries down his collection
of radioactive elements: two milligrams of radium
and a crate of uranium nitrate he stows under a workbench.

Soon he boils and filters pitchblende,
an ore that may hold twenty elements.
He pours solutions, filters and crystallizes salts
he puts under a microscope.
While Otto is patient with details,
Lise looks beneath or beyond for patterns.
She builds an electroscope from a mirror,
old coffee and tobacco cans, a magnifying glass,
and layers of tinfoil.
As she sets a substance to examine under the glass,
the foil leaves flap up or flutter down, quickly
or slowly depending on the electric or radioactive charge.

From early morning past evening, Lise works
in a building with no women's bathroom.
Around midday, she puts on her hat and coat
and heads to a café. Every time she walks down
streets named after German scientists and poets,

she sees some beauty: a man playing a violin
standing by a hat filled with coins, a child picking up a pebble.
Every time she passes round marble-topped tables
to enter the public restroom, she is reminded
she's not quite a part of a scientific team.

Before returning to the basement laboratory,
Lise tiptoes up the forbidden stairway, through
corridors that smell like hot glue and roasted peanuts.
At the back of the lecture hall, she ducks
behind chairs filled with men. Her skirt
cushions her knees as she listens.

Rules

Physicists slide through the street-level windows
rather than walking around to the door
and down the steps to Lise and Otto's laboratory.
James Franck and Max von Laue are so curious
about their colleagues' findings they seem to forget
a lady is in the room. Still, Lise speaks stiffly
so no one interprets friendliness as flirtation.
If she talks lightly, she might not seem serious.
If she sounds too confident, she might be called bold.

Before shops close each evening, she or Otto
dash out to buy cheese or salami and black bread
to carry home later. If they were seen
eating together, rumors of intimacy might rise.
Some evenings Otto heads to a cabaret or dance hall.
Lise returns to the house where she rents a bedroom,
shares a kitchen and bathroom with elderly women.
A line of light blinks on from under one shut door,
a reminder that good women don't wander in the night.

Lise washes up in the shared bathroom
strung with drying lingerie looping like fishing nets.
Then she turns on the small lamp in her bedroom.

She reads math books until she falls asleep,
wakes from a dream of beautiful equations.

The Greenhouse

After the university opens to women,
a bathroom is built in the chemistry building.
Now Lise can freely go up and down stairs.
She smiles at new students on campus.
A woman her age introduces herself.
Elisabeth Schiemann's face pinkens with pleasure
as she talks about fungi mutations and genetics.

Elisabeth shows Lise the university gardens.
She wears a fresh flower tucked in her dress,
which is more flowy than fitted so she can easily kneel
with a spade, clippers, or magnifying glass.
Her hands are determined and delicate as bee wings
as she scrapes strawberries for samples
she smears on small glass plates.

In the greenhouse, she steps aside to let Lise look
under the microscope at thin spiraling strands.
Nothing may replace the sweetness of wild berries,
but we aim to make new varieties
that are easier to match on top of cakes.

Elisabeth's smooth blond hair is swept back.
Her mouth and nose might be called dainty
if they weren't wrinkled into resolve.
She says, *A strawberry is a strawberry. But if
you change one part, something can be lost.*

Names

Otto smooths his waxed mustache
and puts on his overcoat to go dancing.
Lise bends over a desk to check his calculations,
which show heat rising staggered
like a stairway, not sloping like a hill.
The math is like the twisted threads on the back
of embroidered pictures that widen with each stitch.
She writes about how alpha scattering
increases with the atomic mass of metallic elements.
This is their ninth collaboration. All their papers
were published with Otto's name above hers.
It's customary to put the best-known name first.

Lise signs reports of studies she did alone
using her first initial: Dr. L. Meitner.
An impressed editor requests more articles,
but retreats after learning the author is not a *Sir*.
Lise sells articles elsewhere. She also earns money
translating French or English reports into German.
The pay isn't enough to stop taking a stipend
from her father, which she carefully measures
to buy bread, tea, cigarettes, and the daily newspaper.

Hidden

Lise takes the eight-hour train ride to see her family
on holidays. Her father, who's unwell, hopes
his youngest son will take over his law practice one day.
But Walter tells Lise he wants to study chemistry.

She finds some of her old books for him
and shows Robert, now five, the periodic table
in the book her father gave her.
Since she inked in *Ra* for radium,
other elements have been discovered,
and much about atoms. She tells Robert,
Each element is made of just one kind of atom.
That word means: "what cannot be divided."
Once people thought nothing could be smaller.
Now we know atoms are made of smaller parts.

Science is beautifully built on facts,
but some shift as knowledge grows.
Lise runs a finger over rare earths
that are radioactive, listed at the bottom.
What's hidden may have more power
than what we see.

I like that row best, Robert says.

Me too. Especially the empty squares.
Some elements are waiting to be found.

The Front of the Room

SALZBURG, AUSTRIA, 1909

Otto reads aloud reports on their collaborations
at colloquiums, since he enjoys public speaking.
But more and more, Lise speaks up
in the discussions that follow.
She publishes papers using her whole name now.
She reads them aloud in Berlin,
at other universities in Germany,
then in her home country. In Salzburg,
she stands at a podium. Her breath betrays her,
but after her first few sentences, words flow whole.
She compares alpha particles,
the least penetrating form of radiation,
to beta particles and gamma rays,
the most energetic form of invisible light.
In the front row, Max Planck proudly smiles.

A Pitcher of Cream

Later that afternoon, Max says, *We'll hear*
a young man who's making more sense
of my quantum physics than I ever found.

Albert Einstein's dark hair spirals.
His eyes shine like deep pools.
He speaks of his equation: $E = mc^2$.
Mass multiplied by the speed of light,
an enormous number, then squared,
or multiplied by itself, equals the energy of that body.
This is science, not alchemy. No lead is turned into gold.
But it seems that something as simple as a spoon,
and energy, which might spin that solid spoon,
aren't opposite. One can be the other.

After the lecture, Max and Lise walk by the Danube.
They stop in a shop where she buys a green felt hat
with a feather in the band to bring back to Otto.
Max hopes to lure Einstein to Berlin. *He works*
in Switzerland now but was born in Germany.
Surely he'd be delighted to return to the Fatherland!

The next day Marie Curie lectures. Afterward,
Max introduces her to Lise in a small group.

Lise feels shy in front of the genius,
so turns to help pass around cups of coffee.
Marie Curie's gray eyes stop on her
as if to say one of the two woman scientists
in the room is putting herself
in danger of disappearing.
Lise sets down the pitcher of cream.

The Whole Picture

Otto heats samples of various elements
that color flames differently.
Copper casts a green shine. Calcium shows up as orange.
Lise identifies elements by noting
each particular wavelength of light.
Radioactivity clarifies how atoms
may break up and change into other elements
in less than an eyeblink or over thousands of years.
When watching lasts months, they take turns at night,
with Otto napping with his green hat over his face.
Or they sing duets of Brahms songs to stay awake.

Lately, Otto often leaves early to dance
with Edith, an art student he's courting.
Lise sits through the night by the Geiger counter
she made from a hollowed-out brick,
an empty pill bottle, and caps of mechanical pencils
with the ends sawed off to make tubes.
As an element changes form, alpha particles strike
metal plates, making a pulse measured by clicks.
She counts as carefully as her grandmother taught her
over small stitches that build a whole picture on cloth.

Three Green Plates

Lise stands by her father's gravestone
marked with the word "humanitarian."
Memory may be prayer, twining past and present
like the two candles her grandmother lit on Friday nights.

The family returns to the rooms where Lise grew up.
She and her sisters help their mother pack
as she prepares to move to a smaller apartment.
Gusti tells Lise she should move back to Vienna
to help her. Unmarried daughters have duties.
Lise is glad when Robert interrupts.

Tante Lise, look what I made!
Robert shows her an alarm clock he fashioned
from scavenged bolts, pins, gears, and springs.
Sparks nudge a revolving metal dial
against an electromagnet, which clangs at the set time.
While Lise asks him questions, she hears
Gusti and their sisters argue about the piano.

Mutti whispers, *Lise, your father was proud*
you kept and carry on our name. I'll be fine on my own,
but I'm sorry I won't be able to send a monthly stipend.

She gives Lise three green glass plates,
all that's left from a set they used for breakfast,
and Omi's sewing box, with the scissors shaped like a bird.
We gave away your father's law books, Mutti says.
Apparently they weren't worth much anymore.

Tears warm Lise's eyes. Grief for the books
gone and her father, who believed that law by law
the world moves closer to justice.
She runs her hand over her mother's hair,
wrinkled and gray like a lake in a storm.

Tag

On Sunday afternoons, Max Planck invites friends
to his grand house. Max is pleased his daughters
aspire to be good wives, but worries that his sons
seem aimless, moving from one job to another.
Erwin's trousers are tucked into his socks, forgotten
after keeping them from catching on bicycle chains.
Karl scratches the ear of an orange cat.

Max convinced Albert Einstein to move to Berlin,
offering an impressive salary not to teach
or run experiments, but to think.
Today he brought his violin, but not his sons or wife,
a physicist who Lise expects would want to meet others.
I hear their marriage is not strong, Elisabeth whispers.

Max's thinning hair looks as stiff as his starched collar.
He spreads his pale fingers over the piano keys
while his daughters sing. Erwin plays the cello.
Einstein tucks his instrument under his chin.
His rumpled clothes look like they were plucked
from the floor of a bigger man's bedroom.
He lifts a bow, stirs a too-thin tone.

Afterward, everyone walks outside to the rose garden,
where Lise talks with Max's twin daughters.
She's close enough in age to Emma and Grete
that they confide about sweethearts,
but old enough that they don't expect
her to divulge romances of her own.

As the late afternoon spins gold over the garden,
Max calls, *Let's play tag!*
Lise's skirt fans just below her knees
as she twirls past green wicker chairs,
hawthorn and cherry trees.
Her wrist burns where Erwin lightly tags her.
How long has it been since she was touched?

Snapdragons

To celebrate Elisabeth's PhD in genetics,
Lise brings strawberries in a yellow bowl
to the house that Elisabeth and her sister rent
from family friends. They let Elisabeth plant
in the backyard and store tools in an old shed.
Outside, stalks bend under the weight
of stacked small dragon-like faces. Lise asks,
Why do you study snapdragons instead of other flowers?

Mixing seeds from a red snapdragon with seeds
from white ones can turn blossoms pink, Elisabeth says.
They don't follow the genetic laws of dominance,
but blend colors instead of choosing one.
We can learn about heredity, not just in flowers.
How is your work going?

Lise talks about the mesothorium she and Otto isolate.
We hope it can replace radium at less cost.
Radium is put into pills and tonics for good health
or toothpaste for shine. It's added to paint
so watch dials, doorbells, buckles on slippers,
and pajama buttons glow in the dark. Most importantly,
radium burns through tumors in skin or organs.

Some speculate that radiation could help power ships
or light a city someday. Lise looks into the unseen,
a search with its own momentum.
Someone else can decide how to use what she finds.

Shadows

Another woman lectures at the weekly physics colloquium.
After Eva von Bahr's talk on infrared radiation,
she tells Lise, *Max invited me to stay and work here.*
He can't offer a salary, which I didn't have
in Sweden, either. Women aren't allowed
to teach at universities there, but they called me
an exception. Until the professor who hired me died.
Then people acted as if I'd never been around.

The word "exception" can shift to mean "unnecessary."
Lise knows that if her observations
are ever less than stellar, men might say:
We tried including a woman, but it didn't go well.

Names of Birds

Around noon, Lise and Eva walk to the park
with its tidy flower beds and pebbled paths.
Vendors sell paper cones of sunflower seeds
that Eva scatters for sparrows and wrens.
Like their wing feathers, her blunt-cut hair
and short eyelashes are pale brown.
Sitting on green benches, the friends
unfold paper from sandwiches.
They talk about the alpha particle studies
Eva is doing with James Franck. After years
of discussing radiation, this is the first time
Lise has done so while eating lunch.
The pumpernickel bread and cheese are delicious.

Some summer weekends, the friends hike in nearby forests.
Eva tells Lise the Swedish names of magpies,
woodpeckers, and doves. *I miss Sweden's mountains,*
she confides. *Don't you ever get lonely? Or homesick?*

Yes. Lise visits her family on holidays
but misses ordinary moments, like seeing
what Robert is doing in math. *But I'm grateful
to work with Otto. This isn't research I can do alone.*

I'd be happier with a roommate, Eva says.
If you moved in with me, you can just pay what you can.

I won't be much help in the kitchen. Lise looks up
as clouds shift and break apart into the blue.
But I've seen your stacks of books.
I'm handy with nails and a saw. I can build shelves.

Doors

Lise and Otto are promised work in a research center
being built. The Kaiser Wilhelm Institute
is named after Germany's emperor
but privately funded by companies who expect
scientists to focus on practical projects they can use.
Fritz Haber will head one branch
and Emil Fischer another. Emil puts Otto in charge
of Germany's first radioactivity laboratory.
Lise, who worked alongside Otto for five years,
is given a position as an unpaid guest researcher.

She doesn't want to complain.
She was taught that a woman must appear
not to need money, food, or anger,
which can be part of ambition.
She can skip lunch, maybe supper, though
her stomach growls while she and Otto
order laboratory doors easily opened with elbows,
instead of touching and turning knobs.
She's grateful for work in air uncontaminated
by old studies that could skew results.

Otto says, *I invited Edith to stop by to see this place.*
He introduces a blond woman with a heart-shaped face.

When Lise asks her about art school, Edith says,
I like portraits, but noses are hard to get right.
Mostly I paint still lifes. Vases, jars, candlesticks.
She blushes when Otto says, *I expect*
she'll have more than art to keep her busy soon.

Shine

Otto's usually steady hands shake as he scrapes
a tiny sample of mesothorium onto the velvet cushion
of a small box that seems meant to hold a ring.
He tells Lise, *Now that I'll get paid here as well*
as my small university salary, I can propose.
My mother left me her wedding ring.
It's all I have of hers, so I want to keep it.
Besides, Edith might like something more modern,
though she's not an independent sort like you.

You could ask her what she wants. Lise glances down.

After I mentioned my intentions to Emil Fischer,
he talked to the trustees. Otto's eyes widen.
They said they'd build us a house down the street.
They don't want their director of radiation studies far away.

Soon there's a parade to celebrate the institute's opening.
Kaiser Wilhelm II's cloak billows over his uniform
and the sword at his hip.
His waxed mustache and polished boots shine.
Inside the building whose name is already shortened
to KWI, Otto dims the lights so Kaiser Wilhelm

can appreciate mesothorium's glow.
He introduces the emperor to Lise.

Die Mitarbeiterin? The kaiser nods,
then sweeps out of the laboratory.
Gold tassels stream from his cloak.

He called me your assistant! Lise's face burns.
Surely he was told we're a team!

Of course, Otto says. *I suppose he assumed . . .*

No one makes sure I have a house. I don't get a salary.
I love this work, but a person needs money to live on.
Trying to steady her voice, Lise switches on the lights.
Max stands in the doorway. His spectacles glint.

Belonging

Five years ago Max Planck told Lise
that good women are devoted to children, kitchens, and church.
Now he offers a job never before given
to any woman in Germany. As the professor's paid assistant,
Lise sets up experiments and grades 143 assignments
each week. When Max is away or ill, she lectures
on mechanics, thermodynamics, and kinetic theory.

Emil Fischer notices. The man who once forbid
her from going upstairs in the Chemistry Institute
now offers a salary at KWI. Otto will oversee
chemistry in the radioactivity lab, while she heads
the physics division of the Laboratorium Hahn-Meitner.

Abracadabra

Soon after Otto and Edith marry, Otto and Lise
find a substance that might fill an empty square
in the periodic table.
To prove it's a new element,
they pulverize uranium ore for samples
Otto boils in nitric acid,
then chemically separates and purifies.
Lise examines its spectra, and measures
the range and patterns of alpha particles.

After more than a year of work, Otto waves his green hat
over some silica residue and bows. *Here it is!*
But the next day they triple-check calculations.
Otto mutters, *Ach, false claim.*
They call what they seek *abracadabra,*
while considering a permanent name honoring a place,
Greek idea, or person from the past. Otto suggests,
We could name it after ourselves. Lisotto.

The team moves forward on confidence.
Humility nudges them to look again. At last
Otto puts down a vial, hums a Brahms song.
Lise sings along, blending in two-part harmony.

She says, *Let's run the experiment another time or two.*
We can't publish unless we're certain.

The decay process may take another two years!
We'd risk someone else claiming our discovery first.

That's better than publishing and getting it wrong.
Lise knows some scientists mocked Otto
for calling mesothorium a new element,
not recognizing it as a variation,
but most respect the work he's done before and after.
A woman could be exiled because of one wrong claim.

Marching

Flyers are tacked onto posts and bandstands.
A boy shouts, waving a newspaper.
Lise gives him a coin and reads
the headlines declaring war.
On her way to the university she passes
kiosks of newspapers, statues of German musicians,
artists, philosophers, and Victory, a woman
balancing on a column studded with gilded cannons.
She meets Max, who's proud that his sons will now
have a purpose, *Serving the glory of Germany.*

Soon Lise, Edith, Elisabeth, and Eva go to the train station.
Children wave small flags. Young women hand
chocolates to infantrymen or slip roses into their rifles.
Elisabeth sways and claps in time to drums.
All but Eva cheer for the soldiers,
whose gray sleeves cover half their gloved hands.
*In Sweden we don't dress up nutcrackers
as if ready for battle,* Eva murmurs.
We haven't had a war in a hundred years.

Germans want peace, but we were provoked

and must defend our borders. Elisabeth's voice
is stiff. Her white dress billows around her legs.

At least the war will be short, Lise says.
The kaiser says the soldiers will be back
before the leaves fall from trees.

Einstein is one of the few scientists who didn't enlist.
Eva looks up at sparrows in the trees.
He says German schools train children for the army,
memorizing rules, marching them around classrooms.

Einstein should read more newspapers.
Lise doesn't understand how gunfire will settle
arguments about land, but loyalty matters.

Borders

Signs written in French or English are torn down
as those countries are now Germany's enemies.
Gott strafe England—God punish England—
is stamped on wrapping paper and envelopes.
Otto and many professors and students join the army.
For years Jewish men were kept out of military positions,
called cowards, accusations based on nothing.
But the war means they're now wanted in the army.
Professors James Franck and Richard Willstätter
enlist partly to prove their patriotism.

At the university, desks and chairs are stacked and stored.
Hospital beds are set up in classrooms turned into wards.
Lise and Edith volunteer to dole out medicine,
change bandages, open and shut windows.
Edith sketches soldiers practicing on crutches,
but after a month she puts away her pencils,
tells Lise that Otto worries this work makes her too sad.
We hoped I'd have a baby to keep me company
while he's away in the army, she says.
Otto is afraid the radiation you work with
hurt our chances for a child.

We wash our hands often. Lise curls her fingers.
We painted chairs yellow to be used only by people
who've been close to radioactive materials. We're careful.

Birds and Monuments

The war that people first hoped would end by fall,
then by Christmas, moves through spring
into another summer.
At home, Lise checks the newspaper's black-bordered
columns of names for colleagues or her brothers
and her sisters' husbands. She folds the newspaper,
grateful not to recognize a name. She watches
Eva reach over the potted geraniums to sprinkle
sunflower seeds for chickadees and woodpeckers.
*Did you hear about the chlorine gas that can blind
soldiers or burn their lungs?* Eva asks.
*The wind can blow the gas in any direction,
killing innocents. Birds will drop from the sky!*

Chlorine gas can end the war earlier, saving lives.
Lise repeats what Otto wrote to her, along
with queries about the experiments she continues.

Berlin is filled with monuments to might, Eva says.
I should go back to Sweden. I don't belong here.

*James is counting on you to keep on with the work
you started together,* Lise says. *You can't stop!*

What real good do we do? For all anyone knows,
someone will find a way to use radiation as a weapon.
And I'm not as ambitious as you.

Is that what I am?

Ambition isn't wrong. At least no one
minds it in men. I miss my family and old friends.
What would make you stop?

Not loneliness. Lise's home is science.
No one can take that. She'd dare anyone to try.

Do Not Touch

After Eva leaves, Lise is alone in the apartment
with emptied bookshelves. Only her own dresses
hang from the nails she hammered into the walls.
The laboratory is often empty too, except
when chemists come in to rifle through cigar boxes
looking for screws, corks, glass tubes, or spare wire.

Lise believes she's close to finding a new element,
but certainty may have to wait.
Like James and Richard, she wants to show her loyalty
to the country where she lives, which in war
is united with the country where she grew up.
She takes classes in the medical application of X-rays
and anatomy, trains as a surgery nurse.
Then tenderly runs her palm over the pine table
that holds a Geiger counter, needle-nose pliers,
and small sheets of foil packed inside cigarette tins.
She props DO NOT TOUCH signs on unfinished experiments.

Lise takes a train to a military base.
She walks down roads of slush and brick dust,
past shattered tree trunks, broken buildings.
Working in a wing of an old bell factory converted
to a hospital, she meets George de Hevesy,

a chemist in charge of melting church bells
for copper to make bullets. He hates this work.

Lise mends electrical wiring, solders broken pipes,
becomes known as the hospital mechanic.
She bandages wounds on men who smell faintly like licorice
from the anise used for antiseptic. She hears cries for help
in German, Polish, Russian, and Hungarian.
Screams sound the same in every language.

Doors and Curtains

As Lise assembles X-ray apparatus, a doctor scowls.
We do fine without invisible rays. He means *women.*
She patiently coaxes him to give the machine a try.
You'll do the important part, the surgery,
but won't have to probe for broken bullets or bones,
slice into muscles that don't need to be cut.

Lise tacks dark curtains over windows,
helps a patient from a stretcher onto a table.
She passes a scope over wounds and takes pictures,
standing behind a wooden door
for protection from the rays so small and fast
that they can slip past soft skin or organs,
but are stopped by dense bones or metals.
Her geometry locates a bullet lodged in the bladder,
not the stomach, as the doctor believed.
Quietly a precious life is saved.

Between Battles

Lise's second winter at the war front has begun
when the crack and blast of gunfire fades.
While soldiers leave for other battlefields,
Lise squeezes into a space on a train car
marked PASSENGERS WITH HEAVY LOADS.
Women balance children on their laps
or hunker over baskets of food or all their belongings.
Soldiers step over crutches and knapsacks.
Some wear black armbands to honor lost comrades.

Half the mouth of one infantryman twists like wax.
Others cough, their lungs blistered from chlorine gas
that stained their buttons yellow-green.

Geraniums

The old apartment's windowsill is bare
of sunflower seeds and flowerpots.
Lise finds a small stack of letters from Eva.
Before she can open them, she hears the scrape of wheels.
Elisabeth pushes a wheelbarrow
filled with geraniums in pink bloom
she'd taken to her own apartment to water.

Lise and Elisabeth board a trolley driven
by one of the women who've taken on jobs
men held before the war. On the way to the university,
Elisabeth tells her that one of Max's sons died in battle.
The other is in a military prison.

Max's face looks thinned by grief even as he smiles
at Lise, who tells him she's back on leave.
Please stay here, he says. *Not just to help me
with classes again, which are small with so many
at the front. But someone must carry on science.*

Grace and Interruptions

Lise reads old letters from Eva about a man
she met in the trade school where she now teaches.
Lise travels to Sweden for their wedding.
Eva seems happy with Niklas and with introducing
a new generation of girls to chemistry and physics.
Lise tells her, *You were right. War is wrong.*
Maybe she's unpatriotic, but Lise now cares
more that the war ends than about who wins.

Eva presses her hand. *Lise, I miss you.*
But you can always count on me.
What did she think was going to happen?

Back in Berlin, where food and coal are scarce,
the cold laboratory doesn't feel like home.
Lise is jealous that Elisabeth's research
is considered essential. Since food is no longer
delivered across country borders, Elisabeth is trying
to create new types of barley, potatoes, and grapes
that will grow well despite Germany's cold winters.

Lise keeps on her hat and coat as she examines
the green residue of silica she and Otto isolated.

In the periodic table in the book her father gave her
she writes *Pa #91* in the bottom row.
She wears Otto's Alpine hat while she writes
for publication about protactinium, a silver-gray metal.
Though Otto is still away, she puts his name
in front of hers on the report.
There's more to a discovery than arriving at certainty.
She and Otto began together, wrestled past questions.
The triumph is to work as a team.

Trio

Newsboys shout, *Kaiser Wilhelm gives up the throne!*
Lise reads that the emperor packed his shiny helmet
and fringed cloaks to live in exile in Holland.
She and Elisabeth walk to the large ornate gate
on the edge of Berlin. They stand among tired mothers
and small children, but not many other young women,
who may be at work in factories or fields or uncertain
of how to greet soldiers back from a war they lost.

One Sunday afternoon, Max asks friends to visit.
Much has changed in the peach-colored house.
Everyone mourns Max's younger son and his daughters,
who both died days after giving birth to girls.
Each is named after the mother she lost.
Little Grete crawls under the piano, clutching a toy bear.
Elisabeth bends over baby Emma, covers
her face with her hands, opens them,
says, *Peek-a-boo*, then hides again.

Lise thanks Max's surviving son for his service.
And thank you for your work in the hospital, Erwin replies.
Now I'm looking for a job in government.
Maybe I can help the country get back to normal.

They greet Einstein, James, Richard, and Haber,
who was in charge of developing chlorine gas.
Otto and James worked under his command,
but Richard refused on moral grounds.
Instead, he designed three-layer gas masks for protection.

James's little girl shows Lise the medal
her father won for courage. The Iron Cross is printed
with: THE FATHERLAND WILL ALWAYS BE GRATEFUL.
James says, *At least we showed that Jewish men
are as patriotic as any other Germans.*

*Yes, though my family never joined
a synagogue*, Haber says.

*You may not call yourself Jewish, but cowards
who look for ways to divide people see you that way,*
Einstein says. *It's foolish to try to blend in, to believe
one can swap hiding one's history for safety.*

Max sits at the piano, calls Erwin to get his cello.
Einstein's new wife brings him his violin.
He lifts it to his chin, stirs slightly unsteady notes
that stop Lise's breath. The baby cries.
No one carries her away. Everyone needs her tears.

The River

Lise and Otto are praised for finding a new element.
But there's much more work ahead.
Discoveries aren't endings, but revelations of new layers.
Otto is named the new director of their branch
of KWI, where, though Kaiser Wilhelm fled Germany,
his gold-framed portrait remains in the front hall.
Lise is asked to head a physics laboratory of her own.
A sign by the door reads: LABORATORIUM—LISE MEITNER.

Elisabeth fills jars and flasks with *die Blumen:*
lilies, lavender, snapdragons, wild roses, and mint.
Lise will no longer work as Max Planck's assistant.
She's hired as an associate professor at the university.

To celebrate, Lise, Elisabeth, and her sister
bunch up their skirts and ride bicycles to the river.
They swim until they hear distant thunder.
Elisabeth's sister stays in the water, but Lise
and Elisabeth return to a blanket on the shore.
Bees nudge skin-soft petals on a quest for pollen.

Elisabeth passes Lise a strawberry from a glass jar
she filled. *I'm still trying to crossbreed these,*

but strawberries keep outsmarting me.
Elisabeth watches a red bird fly over a nest.
I'm happy for your successes, Lise. But
I worry I'll never even get paid for my work.

Gertrud wades out of the water.
She picks up a camera and takes a photo of Lise
and Elisabeth, whose hair smells like leaves.
Their bare legs stretch toward the river,
their straw hats tossed to the side.

The Eraser

Lise walks by tents set up in the park
as homes for those who can't afford roofs.
Some men in old uniforms wear patches over their eyes.
Folded, empty sleeves are pinned in place.
Barefoot children in tattered clothes hold empty
cups or tin pails, lining up for milk rations.

The gap between rich and poor stands
as clear as if they're on either side of a shut door.
Shiny automobiles speed around corners
past a blinking traffic light said to be the first in Europe.
Lively cafés, cabarets, and department stores
with escalators and revolving doors open.
Fights sometimes break out in the streets.

Law and order have worsened since the emperor left,
Elisabeth says. *We need real leadership again.*

Women have new freedoms, though, Lise says.
*I probably wouldn't be teaching
at the university if a monarch was still in power.*
She lectures on Einstein's equation suggesting
the deep connection between matter and energy.
Classes are small, as some students never returned

from war. Others can't afford tuition
or are too cold or hungry to study much.
The physics department has no funds to buy books
from other countries, so Lise recruits students
to copy books in their best penmanship.

Lise writes another equation on the blackboard,
but in the middle drops her hand holding chalk,
asks, *Where should we go now?*
She wants students to understand
they'll be baffled more than confident,
to find pleasure in heading to the unknown.

The Back of a Painting

Women bend, stretch, leap over hurdles,
and pull themselves up to their chins on a bar.
Hildegard Rosbaud, a woman with thin-plucked eyebrows,
leads exercise classes in a big room at KWI.
Afterward, Edith invites her and Lise
to walk down the street to her house for coffee.

Lise wants to get to work but understands
Edith needs company. Otto has told her she's melancholy
after many failed attempts to have a baby.
Their dining room is almost as big as the apartment
Lise took down the street in a new building.

The friends dip radishes in salt, eat black bread
spread with butter and sprinkled with chopped chives.
They talk about how Hildegard can keep teaching
exercise classes at KWI, though budget cuts
ended her husband's X-ray research there. Hildegard says,
Paul is happy with his new job editing science magazines.
But Lise feels a chill at the thought of a laboratory
taken away. A scientist must appear irreplaceable.

I took Otto to a gallery last weekend, Edith says.
He hated the blue horses and portraits

with eyes where ears should be.
He said they looked like they were painted by lunatics.

But they're not. Lise looks at the painting
Edith gave Otto for their wedding:
A stack of books without titles. An empty vase.
Why did you stop painting?

Some things just go away. No one knows why.
Edith takes down the painting and turns it to the wall.

Frau Professor Meitner

Lise strides past rows of students with the slightly stiff
posture of being the only woman in the hall.
But there's no sting now as she steps
on a potato crate set behind the lectern.
As the first woman to be named a full professor
in physics at the University of Berlin,
she makes her voice large.
She swears to always pursue truth
and advance the honor of science.
Her words about cosmic physics waft to the back of the hall,
where she once ducked behind chairs to listen.

After Lise accepts congratulations from many,
she greets Elisabeth, who stood by some reporters
taking notes on skinny pads.
Elisabeth unfastens a white rose by her collar.
She pins it under the Belgian lace Lise wears.
I'm proud of you. Elisabeth whispers, *You're beautiful.*

Lise doesn't believe that
until she says, *You are beautiful too.*

Spinning

Three years ago Max Planck won a Nobel Prize.
Now Albert Einstein wins one for his theories
about the thrilling speed of light, the baffling bend of time
that may waffle past clocks, wrinkle and warp space.
Lise watches silent newsreels, shown around the world,
which celebrate the man with wild photogenic hair.

But fame can spin around. The Berlin Philharmonic Hall
fills to hear a speaker who calls Einstein a fraud.
He rants against what he calls Jewish physics.
His supporters pass out leaflets that claim Einstein's theory
of relativity is a Semitic plot advocating chaos.
After these men start scuffles, the public lecture
Einstein was scheduled to give is canceled.

It's for his safety, Elisabeth says. *Those people
insult him because they don't understand his ideas.*

No one understands his ideas. Except maybe Max,
Lise says. *Einstein should speak despite the protests.
Not going gives the hoodlums what they want.
They're some of the same who spread the lie
that Germany lost the war because of Jewish traitors.*

Nobody believes that foolishness.
Unhappy people look for someone to blame.
It's best to pay them no mind.

I just wish people wouldn't make up things
and call them fact. Lise frowns.
There's rot in the lie that one group of people
is worse than others. Any lie sets a space for more.

The Promise

Lise, Edith, and Otto stand between pews and a pulpit.
Edith looks tired and triumphant as she hands
the baby she calls a miracle to Otto.
He kisses him, then passes Hanno to his godmother.
Lise looks down at his pale eyelashes
blinking over blue eyes.

After the christening, they stroll to Max's home.
Lise chats with Hildegard, who holds her little girl.
Lise then walks over to Edith, who shifts the baby
in her arms, winces, clutches him as if afraid he'll fall.
The baby hiccups into tears.
Edith's face collapses. *I'm tired.*

Of course you are. Lise takes Hanno
from her arms. *It's all right. Babies cry.*

But mothers aren't supposed to. Edith runs
the back of her hand over her eyes.

You'll be a good mother. Lise touches
the soft, light hair of the child
she promised to love forever.
His small fists are as soft and warm as porridge.

Bees

Lise's laboratory must be spotless,
but Elisabeth's research allows
for dirt and chance, depends on sunshine.
Lise visits her in the university garden.
Elisabeth pushes apart the snapdragons'
soft petals and guides pollen past them.
She sets down her tweezers, reaches into a basket
for scraps of silk cut from an old petticoat.
She wraps tiny kerchiefs around each blossom.
So bees don't interfere with our experiments.
She snatches a bee in the way of her work,
then opens her hand behind her back to free it.
We move pollen as they do, but keep data.

Your parents must be proud of your work.

My father thought it was sweet when I was a little girl
picking daisies. Even later, planting
a flower bed seemed appropriately feminine.
But once microscopes got involved, he turned his back.
I embarrass the distinguished professor of history.
Elisabeth curls her fingers. *My mother complains*
I've ruined my hands. I tell them genetics is practical.

We show ways for people to grow more food,
make nicer gardens, and improve the human race.

Lise catches her breath hearing the last goal.
It's one thing to decide what's best for plants,
another to aim to change people.

Goodness, we don't try to change anyone.
But it may be merciful to see that fewer ill
or feeble-minded babies are born.

Like Anna?

That sweet girl who empties the wastebaskets? No!
Elisabeth's forehead wrinkles. *There's nothing wrong*
with wanting a generation to be fit and smart.
My adviser says we're in danger of becoming
a nation of snapdragons, with too much crossbreeding.

Lise wraps her arms around herself.
But you love pink snapdragons.

More Than One

Lise takes a train, then a ferry, to Copenhagen, Denmark.
Orange, violet, pale green, and yellow houses
are straight and close together as piano keys.
She walks down cobblestone streets to a stucco building
brightened with flower boxes and a red tile roof.
She's here to lecture and listen at a conference
in the Institute for Theoretical Physics, headed
by Niels Bohr. He used spectral lines to show
how the electrons in atoms may jump between orbits
in quantum leaps, losing or gaining energy.

Lise joins him by a field to watch his sons play soccer.
Amid the boys' shouts, he shakes many hands.
The people of Denmark are so proud
of their Nobel Prize–winning scientist,
they had the institute built in his honor.
Niels is beloved for his kindness, too,
which goes beyond the country's borders.
The Great War ended, but many still think
of Germans as enemies. Niels welcomes everyone.
He believes science should be shared.

Soon Lise steps behind the podium. She looks out
at a distinguished audience that includes Marie Curie.

Lise stumbles over her first three words.
Then she leans into her topic
of the nuclear processes of X-rays and gamma rays.

After the applause, she greets George de Hevesy,
who she met during the war when he melted church bells.
Here in Copenhagen, he and Dirk Costner
recently discovered an element they call hafnium,
in honor of the ancient name for the city's safe harbor.

Lise then talks with Irène Curie abut whether
it's possible to not only find new radioactive elements,
but to create them. Irène's mother joins them.
They both have gray eyes and red, roughened hands.

Marie Curie congratulates Lise
on her talk and the discovery of an element.
Merci, Lise replies, feeling giddy. *Thank you. Danke.*
Einstein comes over along with a few men
he introduces, saying, *Lise Meitner is our Marie Curie.*

Lise is both flattered and annoyed.
If women scientists must be measured,
why not against the men in the room
rather than the first person to win two Nobel Prizes?
Most men aren't geniuses, but do necessary work.
No one expects every man to be like Pierre Curie.

Lise carries Marie Curie's name like a torch.
But surely there's room for more than one
woman scientist on a continent or in a century.

The Stand

Science is not as solitary as history may make it seem.
And colleagues who challenge, collaborate,
or compete often live in other countries.
Lise packs her suitcase, the color of dusty corn,
and lectures in Zurich, London, Brussels, Rome,
and back home in Vienna, where she sees Gusti
and Robert, who now studies physics at the university.

Lise returns to Germany. After she lectures in Munich,
Richard Willstätter gives her a bouquet of yellow roses.
Over dinner they talk about KWI, where before the war
he planted tulips and dahlias to study pigments.
Richard left Berlin seven years ago to teach
at the university in Munich. He recently resigned.
He explains, *They turned down three well-qualified*
chemists for a position, saying there are enough
Jewish professors here. I had to take a moral stand.

On Lise's way to the train station to head home,
she buys a set of colored pencils for Hanno,
though Otto says he wishes Edith wouldn't encourage him
to draw. Boys already tease him for being small.

Lise carries the pencils and roses back to Berlin.
She visits Elisabeth in her apartment,
where she's stitching wavy blue lines
along the neckline of one of her white dresses.
Beside her, another dress soaks in a tin tub by a box
of Persil powder that promises: *To wash white as snow.*

We heard Richard resigned, Elisabeth says.
*They say every student in the hall stood
and clapped and clapped after his last lecture.*
She puts down her needle. *I don't understand
what good it does to lose an esteemed professor.*

If no one speaks up, those in the wrong can get stronger.

Perhaps, but we should be practical, too,
Elisabeth replies. *Now Richard
doesn't have a job, and I don't expect any
of those three worthy chemists were hired.*

Lise picks up a book written by Elisabeth's adviser.
He's famous for developing eugenics,
studying genes to increase traits he calls desirable.
*I can't say what Professor Baur intends,
but it's certainly not to create more people
like my grandparents who escaped from massacres.*
She shuts her mouth before saying, *And me.*

You mean because they were Jewish?
Our genetics research has nothing to do with religion.

I wasn't raised to follow a religion.
But I believe all lives have worth.

I think that too! Elisabeth turns her face
as if she were slapped. She swallows
and picks up another book. *That's not all I study.*
We were taught that fields were first planted here
in Germany, but I'm starting to think
that barley and wheat were first planted south of here,
where summers are longer. Perhaps even in Africa.

How can scientists learn where agriculture began?
Lise is glad to change the subject.
She doesn't want to fight, not with Elisabeth.

Signs that plants were used many ways
—eaten raw or roasted, taken as medicine or used
in rituals—suggest they've been around a long time.
Shucking barley goes faster when the kernels are big.
Finding seeds of various sizes would be a sign
that people were trying to improve on grains found in the wild.
That may be where fields were first planted.

Seeds

James Franck and his wife leave for Stockholm, where
he'll collect a Nobel Prize for his electron studies.
Lise stands with their teenaged daughters in a crowd
of devoted students and friends who cheer
as the train leaves the station.

When James returns, a smaller group gathers at Max's home.
The teenagers stand in the winter-bare garden, sharing shawls.
Some children find enough snow to shape small houses.
A boy runs from the kitchen with a teacup
full of breadcrumbs to lure birds.
Lise and Elisabeth go into the parlor, where a girl reads
under a table holding a silver urn, cheese, and apple strudel.
They greet guests—Max, Einstein, Haber—
who also have gold medals engraved with their names.

Lise and Elisabeth talk with Hertha Sponer, who's tall,
blond, and serene. She worked with James after Eva left.
Now back from a fellowship in California, Hertha supervises
two hundred students in studies of molecular spectra.
She admires the gold medal propped on the mantelpiece
and tells Lise, *You and Otto should have gotten one
for discovering protactinium.*

Lise will win a Nobel Prize yet. Elisabeth nods
as a man steps in to talk with Hertha,
then whispers to Lise, *Am I the only one
here who's not a physicist or chemist?*

We appreciate biologists, too. Lise plucks small sandwiches
from a tray. She hands one to Elisabeth. *Who else
might remind us of the marvels of wheat, rye, and barley,
grasses that made bread and civilization possible?*
The tall clock chimes. Its pendulum swings.

We should know more about where they first grew,
Elisabeth says. *I'd really like to look
for ancient seeds in deserts that were once green.*

You've been talking about Egypt all year, Lise says.
Go. You can count on me to water your plants.

October Evening

Elisabeth and Lise ride bicycles to an orchard
and pick apples. Elisabeth puts some in a blue bowl
on her kitchen table. Lise sets some aside
to bring to her nephew. She's proud and happy
that after earning a PhD in Vienna, Robert now
works in the University of Berlin's physics department.

Elisabeth's apartment is quiet, with her sister
at a concert where a friend is playing the piano.
Elisabeth talks about her recent research trip to Egypt
and the Middle East. She explored old tombs,
dug up clay vessels that survived for centuries
with imprints of stalks, leaves, grapes, and vines.
She brought back seeds to inspect their genes
and examine links between wild and cultivated plants.

*There's evidence that civilization began under the hands
of people with dark skin,* she says. *Some of my colleagues
at the botanical gardens call me unpatriotic to say so.
And they refuse to believe that women, who long gathered berries,
nuts, and roots, probably planted the first gardens.*

You need different colleagues. Lise is glad Elisabeth's focus
is shifting from the genes of people to those of plants.

*True. When I finish my book about the origins of plants,
maybe I'll be hired as a full professor at the university.
Where you teach. Where my father taught.*

*Sadly it takes some administrators a while
to recognize talent, especially in women,* Lise says.
*Hedwig Kohn taught in Breslau for more than fifteen years
before they named her a full professor.*

*Now with Hertha Sponer and you, Germany can claim
three women physics professors. The world can change!*

Yes! And your time will come. Lise leans
toward Elisabeth. *Now finish writing that book.*

Sugar Cookies and Newspapers

Evergreen wreaths brighten doorways.
The bakery window is filled with Christstollen,
marzipan pigs, and butter cookies shaped
like policemen, stars, and pine trees.
Lise and Elisabeth stop in a bookshop,
Lise chooses a book about pirates
to give Hanno for Christmas.
Elisabeth blushes as she sees two copies
of *The Origin of Cultivated Plants*,
with her name on the cover. Lise buys both,
though Elisabeth gave her a copy.
She tells the owner, *You should order more.*
The author has many admirers.

The women head back to their neighborhood
where children stamp or slide across patches of ice.
A mother calls them in from winter's early darkness.
Lights flicker on in houses.
Inside Elisabeth's apartment, they take off
their coats and boots. Elisabeth gets out sacks of sugar
and flour, a block of butter, to mix batter for cookies.
Lise makes a fire in the hearth, sets the match

back beside candles shaped like gnomes and angels.
She rifles through a newspaper she puts down
when Elisabeth slips a tray into the oven.
It seems the Nazi Party is growing.

Who are they again? Elisabeth asks.

They say they want law and order, but cheer on
thugs who swing iron rods in the streets.
They're a small group. Lise hears the fire crackle.
Adolf Hitler is running for office.

I saw pictures. With that mustache barely
wider than his nose. They say he's quite a clown.
Elisabeth turns back to the oven, pulls out a tray.
I left some soft since that's how you like cookies best.

Lise crushes the newspaper, tosses it into the hearth.
The paper flares, darkens, and shivers into ash.

A New Year

Elisabeth's apartment smells of oranges and damp wool.
Boots stand in snowmelt by the door.
At the kitchen table, Elisabeth takes notes
on the patterns of barley's kernels.
Working beside her is a pleasure, like sitting in the sun.
Lise plans a class on atomic physics and chemistry
she'll co-teach with Leo Szilard.
That should mean half the work,
but while Leo is brilliant, he's undependable,
heading off to London or Paris if he hears rumors
of intriguing experiments.
Lise heard he keeps a packed suitcase by the door.

While the big radio plays classical music,
she opens mail she brought from KWI.
Lise agreed to take on Otto's work heading
their branch while he teaches at a university
in New York this semester. She murmurs,
There's more paperwork than I thought.

Edith didn't want to go to America?

Hanno is nine, a hard age to take him out of school.
But Otto means to travel to California
when classes end. They may join him in summer.
And maybe I'll visit Robert in Rome.
He got a Rockefeller grant to study with Enrico Fermi.
Lise leans closer to the wicker and lacquered wood radio
as words from the new chancellor break the music.
She tilts back as his voice rises to a screech.

He sounds none too intelligent, Elisabeth says.

It's stunning he won the election. Though I read
votes were counted with more folly than truth.
Lise's match snaps as she lights a cigarette.
I don't suppose one person can do much damage.

Together

Lise and Elisabeth weave a way through
crowded sidewalks loud with drumbeats and
the stamp of boots worn by men marching four across.
They wear brown uniforms and armbands
with swastikas, black broken crosses.
They swing their arms in sharp, straight lines.

Spectators squeal, scream, raise their arms
with fingers flat, not grabbing, not reaching,
but giving themselves up—to what?
Lise steps through wood chips and sawdust.
Looking up, no branches bend beneath the sky.
What happened to the linden trees?

The chancellor ordered those on this street
to be cut down to make more room
for everyone watching the parade.
Elisabeth claps in time to the drums,
says, *Marching lifts the spirit.*

Women lean over windowsills, waving handkerchiefs.
Mothers hold up babies to see
the new chancellor with his blue-gray eyes
and a short mustache half-hiding wide nostrils.

Little girls and boys flap paper flags,
mimic the marchers' goose steps, lifting their legs,
then snapping them back down. Some chant along:
Germany, wake up! The Jews are coming!

Elisabeth stops walking, touches Lise's wrist.
The children don't know what it means.

Inheritance

Professors who once greeted Lise
with a friendly *Guten Tag* or *Guten Morgen*
now raise rigid arms and huff *Heil Hitler.*
She crosses the street to avoid them, hurries
into her office at the university. Opening the mail,
she finds a questionnaire for all professors
to complete. They're asked their grandmothers' religion.

Lise never speaks much about where
she comes from, but she doesn't hide it either.
She's shaped by the memories of two candles,
reminders to listen and watch, to remember.
She's heard of people changing their names,
making up family trees, cutting relatives
out of photographs. She'll never do that.
She writes: *Maternal grandmother: Jewish.*
Paternal grandmother: Jewish.

Matter and Energy

Lise strides past double-decker buses,
sleek black cars driven by government men.
She turns her face from men in Hitler's
new black-uniformed Defense Brigade
or Schutzstaffel, shortened to SS.

No children hold tin cups to be filled with milk.
She'd like to think people are no longer thirsty,
but she's afraid the poor and the veterans
with missing legs, arms, or eyes are not gone,
but hidden from view on the clean,
quiet streets the new leaders promised.

Inside the university, much goes on as before.
Where does matter begin? How does it spin into energy?
Lise asks. She shows her advanced students
how to make a cloud chamber by arranging pistons
and tubes to pump moist air into a sealed container.
They photograph the tracks particles leave
in the moist air to study scattering gamma rays
and electrons as they slow down.

Lise and her assistant Max Delbrück co-write
a book about atoms. Radioactivity helps show

the smaller nucleus within each atom.
Protons inside help define its character.
Last year a neutron, a particle with no charge,
was discovered inside the nucleus too.
There's still much to learn about the forces of atoms,
so small, mysterious, and in perpetual motion.

Grandmothers

As Lise tenderly draws together wires
for an experiment, Leo runs in, breathing hard.
A trooper stopped Robert and me at the door.
He told us to go home. A new civil service law
expels Jewish researchers and professors
from public universities. Leo loosens his tie,
glances at her desk, taps an envelope
with a government seal. *Some got letters like that.*

You mean we can't teach our class?
Lise looks at the stack of papers she may never grade.
If she's forced to leave, will someone post a sign
on the classroom door? Will students turn away,
wondering what to do with their books?
Thank goodness Robert plans to go study with Enrico Fermi.

Things aren't safe in Italy either with a fascist in power,
Leo says. *Back in Hungary, when we saw angry people*
with matches, some of us didn't wait around
to see houses set on fire. I'm leaving Germany
while I can. You and Robert should get out too.

Lise is known around the world for discovering an element,
has been nominated for a Nobel Prize six times.
She designed and put together complicated instruments
that show groundbreaking proofs of radioactive recoil
and ways to determine the half-life of radioactive elements.
Surely good work matters as much as her grandmothers.

Boy on a Bicycle

As Lise walks through her neighborhood,
Edith runs out barefooted. She says,
I heard you were told to leave the university.
Otto won't stand for this. He should be here!

I still have a job at KWI. The new laws
only apply where we're employed by the state.
Lise sees a boy steering a bicycle
from behind the house. She waves
to Hanno, who keeps his eyes straight ahead,
intent, she supposes, on balance.

As he turns past lilac bushes, out of sight,
Edith says, *Hanno is upset. His teacher just left.*
Ten is a sensitive age to lose someone you adore.

I'm sorry.

I wrote to Otto about the boycott of shops
and businesses. I had to walk past storm troopers
in brown shirts and black boots to get to my dentist.
As if a Jewish man can't clean teeth as well as anyone.
Edith holds her wrists, but her hands tremble.

I'm sorry. I know things are harder for you.
Hanno's teacher left without even a goodbye.

He'll be all right. Lise shouldn't mind
comforting a friend. But she curls her hand
as if to cool a spark of anger lighting her palm.

The Rope

Sitting at the desk in Otto's KWI office,
Lise opens a government letter demanding
that the institute fly a flag with a swastika.
If Lise doesn't obey,
she may lose the one job she has left.
She draws money from the fund meant
for beakers, solvents, pitchblende, and paper.
She sends Max Delbrück to purchase the flag.
When he comes back, he asks, *Should I raise it?*

No. Nein. It would be cruel to ask someone else
to do what she knows is wrong.
But after Max leaves, she stares at the folded flag
until she hears uneven footsteps. *Hello! Hello!*

Anna tilts as she walks into the room, smiles
as she empties a wastebasket. *My auntie got me
chocolate milk! Do you like chocolate milk?*

Ja, yes, I do. Lise smiles.
After Anna leaves, she carries the flag outside.
She braces against the cold wind, looks away
from the blades of the swastika.

She doesn't pray, but as she pulls the rope,
burns her bare hands,
she silently begs forgiveness.

The Plea

Max Planck invites Lise and James Franck to his garden,
where cherry trees are in pink bloom.
Haber and I were exempted from the dismissals
because of our service in the war, James says.
But I won't stand and speak in front of a class
as if nothing has happened. I resigned.
Haber was ordered to dismiss the Jewish scientists
who work under him. He refused and resigned too.

Please don't leave, Max says.
Reason is bound to come back.

Einstein was right, James says.
They'll never see us as anything but Jewish.
He already resigned from the Academy
of Sciences. He won't come back to Germany.

Einstein is well known, travels, and when asked
about Germany, he can be critical, Max says.
Of course there are problems. No country is perfect,
but we will solve ours without the world watching.

I sent a letter to the newspapers about my resignation,
James says. *To be published outside Germany too.*

Call back that letter, Max says. Bitte. Please.
Our education system is the envy of all Europe.
The chancellor won't let you and Haber—
Nobel Prize winners—go!
I'll talk with him, get right to the point.
I hear he's not gifted at making conversation.

Warnings

Max looks shaken when he returns
from meeting with Hitler. He tells Lise,
I warned him that sending our best scientists away
will only put their knowledge in foreigners' hands.
The veins on his forehead bulged. He yelled
that if dismissing Jews means the end of science,
then we will do without science for a while.
Max squeezes his thin hands together.
Never! We must carry on the ark of science.

Lise imagines people walking in rain,
understanding that land will be covered with deep water,
looking for a mix of animals to make sure
life would go on, if not exactly as before.

Smoke

BERLIN, GERMANY, MAY 1933

The arch topped with a statue of a winged goddess
raising a sword leaves a shadow
like a tall sundial marking time.
On Lise's way to the university to collect
some notebooks left behind, she heads down
streets whose names were changed to honor Nazis.

White blossoms brighten linden trees.
Their sweet fragrance is cut by the smell of smoke.
She thinks of the recent fire in the Reichstag,
which housed Parliament and a library.
Authorities blamed and arrested protesters,
but some whisper that Nazis set the fire
themselves to stir fear and have an excuse
to set new laws ending freedom for people and the press.

Lise walks past black, red, and white banners
hanging from museums and the opera house.
A half-burned book is pierced by a nail
on a post hung with scorched flyers announcing events.
She steps closer to pale orange embers, split book covers,
and strewn spines in mounds taller than horses.
Blackened paper curls like hands into fists.

Lise flinches as an arm circles her waist,
then softens at its familiarity. She murmurs,
They burned hundreds of books, or thousands. Why?
Didn't the police try to stop them? Or professors?

Students and professors were part of the mob,
Elisabeth replies. *When did wisdom become a bad thing?*

Lise scoops up ashes.
Shreds or scraps of paper with lone letters,
edges of words and truths, flutter.
She opens her hands so ashes fall. She runs her palm
over the side of her neat black dress.

Elisabeth bends to wipe off the pale smear,
but Lise steps away.
Everyone should see what was lost.

Colored Pencils

As Lise walks down the street to work,
the postman smiles. Some neighbors
who once looked after one another's
children, plants, or cats turn away.
She tries to avoid Kurt Hess,
who lives in the apartment above hers.
He's the head of organic chemistry at KWI
and now wears an armband with a swastika.

Ringing church bells divide time but leave rough echoes.
Lise sees Hanno sitting on the steps of his house.
When she walks over, he says, *Mutti won't get out of bed.*

Shall I help you make breakfast?
Lise goes inside with him, heats oats
with milk and honey. She sets a blue bowl
on the table, pushes aside stubs of colored pencils,
some broken, or ends that look like they were chewed.
Hanno stares at the porridge. *That's not how Mutti makes it.*

I know.

Soon Hanno heads to school
while Lise goes to work. She writes to Otto:

I'm afraid Edith is falling into melancholy.
Perhaps worse. *I'm sorry I can't be the person*
to make her feel better now. Please cancel
your trip to California. Come back as soon as you can.

Dessert

Otto returns from the United States in July.
He and Edith invite Lise to their house for dinner.
After Hanno leaves the table, the adults
bring coffee to the parlor. Lise picks up a book,
its cover a painting of a path through a marsh.
She believes the technique of dabbing paint
in dots is called pointillism, perhaps inspired
by quantum theories of light.
She slips out a drawing of a cat,
its outline just a few lyrical brushstrokes.

Edith still hopes Hanno will be a painter, Otto says.

He shows talent, Edith says. *And don't expect
his new teacher to encourage science. She told the class
that good Germans evolved from blue-eyed geese.*
Her hand shakes as she lights a candle in a crystal holder.

Dictators hate science. Lise shuts the book.
Facts get in the way of their lies.

Dictator is a strong word, Otto says. *Though
I don't understand why people listen to that fellow.*

Hitler's not smart, or if I might say so, even good-looking.

*Some people admire how he seems like one of them
and cares about them, refusing a salary,* Edith says.

*But he makes a profit selling his hate-filled book.
Mein Kampf has sold a million copies,
partly to our own government,* Lise replies.
They give a special edition to all newlyweds.

My hairdresser lent me a copy, Edith says.
*I don't know why she thought I'd like it. But surely
no one can take seriously a book so horribly written.
I've told Hanno that only ignorant people
claim one race is superior to another.*

Ladies! Otto says. *I leave for a few months
and come home to a new country and my wife
and lab partner talking like revolutionaries.*

The chancellor has said some disturbing things, Lise says.

Ach, he doesn't mean what he says.
Otto puts his hand over Edith's, which still trembles.
*In America, reporters wanted to know
what I thought about the new regime. I assured them*

the German people are wise and good,
that any horrors they heard were exaggerated.

Edith stands up. *I'll bring in the plum tart.*

In the Rose Garden

They say professors must go to Nazi meetings.
Max von Laue and I won't do that. Otto leans forward
on a wicker chair, looking at Max Planck and Lise.
If the university won't hire back our Jewish colleagues,
I'll resign, Otto says. *I've spoken*
to about thirty others who promise to do the same.

Good, good. I won't join the Nazi Party either,
Max Planck says. *But you must understand that*
if those thirty scientists leave, a hundred and fifty others
will be all too glad to take your jobs. And everything
will be worse, especially for our students.
He adjusts his steel-rimmed spectacles.
If you must, take a sabbatical. Do some research.
Things are bound to be back to normal soon.

But what if they get worse? Lise asks.
Some say he wants all Jewish people out of the country.

That's just talk. Even if Hitler meant such threats,
he's too ridiculous to carry them out, Max says.
Golden orioles shriek from the cherry trees.
I'm putting in another nomination for a Nobel Prize

for you both, as I have for the past few years.
Lise, you'll always have work here.

Quiet

As Max warned, James's position is offered
to a man whose science is considered
more in line with national values.
He dismisses Hertha Sponer. She isn't Jewish,
but the Nazis believe women belong at home,
bearing sons for the nation, not taking jobs that could go to men.
Lise learns that Hedwig Kohn was also dismissed.
Now there are no women physics professors in Germany.

At the depot, the train chugs out of sight.
James's devoted friends, colleagues, and students
who cheered when he left to receive a Nobel Prize
are now silent as if at a funeral.
For a few minutes everyone just breathes the smoky air.
Otto says, *I can't imagine leaving the country*
where he was born and raised his daughters.

Some don't have a choice. Lise doesn't add
that thousands of Jewish families are leaving
Germany to be safe. He knows that.
Otto likes to smooth out differences, but she's lucky
to work with a man who's not only excellent at science,
but good. He withdrew from the university
in protest, though he still has work at KWI.

He tells her he's started hiring assistants
to fill in gaps there. *I interviewed many and chose*
the one fellow who didn't say "Heil Hitler."

You should hire Fritz Strassmann, Lise suggests.
He resigned from the Society of German Chemists
when they accepted Nazi policies, though that means
he can neither teach nor work in industry.

Otto is glad to work with the young man,
who's conscientious, cheerful, and too thin.
Fritz says, *I'm grateful for work here,*
though I'd break stones for a living
if it meant I could keep my conscience. I don't miss
being at the university, if we can call it that anymore,
since they dismissed a third of the professors.

Fritz Strassmann and Max Delbrück are among
the dozen young scientists that Lise supervises.
Many of the rest wear armbands with swastikas.
They sometimes dash out of the lab to sing at rallies.
But most seem unenthusiastic, putting up
with Nazi rules to keep their jobs. Lise can't blame them.
There's much she, too, ignores to get on with her work.

Trust

Lise shows her advanced students
how to build a spectroscope by setting
a magnifying lens in a cigar box she paints black.
Light sweeps through slits cut in front of a prism
to a ruled scale that measures wavelengths.
The distinctively colored and patterned bands
whisper the names of elements.

Each Thursday, after her critiques of their experiments,
the students make coffee, pass around
china cups and slices of the apple cake
Lise bought at her favorite bakery.
Most students have left when Anna enters,
listing, weight landing on one foot. *Hello! Hello!*

Lise wraps leftover cake in a linen napkin
and offers it to her. Anna squeals as if it's a holiday,
though Lise gives her cake every Thursday now.
Every Monday Anna brings back the napkin,
Lise believes washed and ironed by her aunt.
Anna tips toward her, collapses into a hug.

Haven

Niels Bohr invites Lise to be a visiting physicist
at the red-roofed institute in Copenhagen.
Lise is glad to leave Germany for a few weeks.
She loves talking with Niels and her nephew Robert,
who was welcomed to research here. His grant
to study in Rome was withdrawn, since fellows
must have jobs to return to, and his in Berlin was taken.
But together they talk with Enrico Fermi,
who's visiting from Rome, and his wife, Laura.

James Franck and Hilde Levi also now work in Copenhagen.
Hilde was granted a PhD back in Berlin just before
the job of her adviser, Professor Haber, was ended.
Young Jewish scientists like her and Robert
would have a hard time finding work if not for Niels.
Now as Hilde pours and passes around coffee,
Lise looks at her as if to say one
of the two women scientists in the room
is putting herself in danger of disappearing.
Hilde sets down the pitcher of cream.

The Passport

In the physics institute library, scientists play Ping-Pong.
Others scribble equations on blackboards or napkins,
talking about how light and atoms are always in motion.
Niels agrees with Einstein that an atom's energy
can't be released, at least not in their lifetimes.
Its nucleus holds most of its weight
and hidden power, like a kernel within a seed.
Niels suggests it might not be hard,
as most thought, but wobble like a liquid drop.

Late in the evening, conversations turn
to the fear that the democracies in Europe are in danger.
James tells Lise he's leaving to teach in the United States.
Maybe you should look for work elsewhere too.
He mentions a women's college in New England
and another in Britain that might need a physics professor.

My spoken English isn't good, Lise says.
She doesn't want to be far away
when Germany returns to normal.
And if it doesn't, all its laws won't apply to her.
She's a citizen of Austria, a free country.
All these years she renewed her passport,
naming the country she comes from, not where she lives.

Rain

That fall Elisabeth leaves Lise a note asking
her to stop by her home. Lise grabs an umbrella,
as it's cloudy, then walks down several streets,
past the old tulip fields and children kicking
a ball, some others tracking the path of a toad.

Elizabeth flings open the door, twirls,
and exclaims, *I got a job as a full professor!*
Her linen dress whirls above her sun-browned legs.

Congratulations! Lise is happy for her, truly,
but Elisabeth must hear her voice thud.
*I know it's not the best time for you to hear this,
Lise. But you know how long I waited.*

*Of course. You weren't the one who ended
my university job.* Lise can't help saying,
I hope yours wasn't taken from someone else.

No! No one in the genetics department is Jewish.

That should tell you something.

Please don't start on that, not today. I study plants.

And you've told me that diversity is how they change.

Yes, strands grow stronger as they adjust to new soil.
Anyway, I don't focus on eugenics,
but must teach basics in my introductory class.
Elisabeth pushes back a strand of pale hair.
Can't you be happy for me?

I am. But I won't ever see your office.
Lise hears rain tap the window.
I can't even step past the pillars at the university.

Don't be dramatic. You've been different
since all this began and it's not fair.
Elisabeth lets out a big breath.
Most Germans don't agree with Hitler's methods,
but he offers peace, a little prosperity.
I know he seems prejudiced and that's wrong.
But they don't mean you.
You don't even celebrate holy days.

Lise knows her friend means well.
She remembers her joy at getting her own laboratory,

which Elisabeth filled with lilies, wild roses, and mint.
At Lise's first lecture as a full professor,
Elisabeth applauded from the back of the room.
I'm proud of you, Lise says. *My apartment is too small
for a party, but if you have guests here, I'll help.*

The Garden Shed

A string of bells jingle on the bakery door.
A plump woman cheerfully says, *Guten Tag, Frau Professor!*
Lise chooses an apple cake, says, *Danke,*
and asks, as always, *How is your little girl?*

Good! The saleswoman grins and folds the cake in paper
as tenderly as if dressing a baby. She carefully creases
the paper and winds it with red-and-white twine
she unspins from a big spool. She blesses
Lise as she puts the wrapped cake into her hands.

It seems lovely until Lise sets it on Elisabeth's table
by a cake Andrea Wolffenstein made,
with waves of chocolate frosting. Women coo
as they discover caramel between the sixth and seventh layers.
Lise drags straw-bottomed chairs into the parlor.
Guests without chairs sit on the floor or on pillows,
some with plates of the seven-layered cake on their laps.
They listen to Andrea play violin, quite perfectly.

During applause and happy chatter
between pieces, Lise steps outside.
Elisabeth joins her by pink snapdragons. Lise says,
I should have brought you a fancier cake and roses.

Andrea is my sister's friend. Elisabeth reaches
into a pocket, pulls out the striped bakery twine.
She playfully loops it over Lise's shoulders.
We can cut some snapdragons. I'll get my clippers.

Lise follows Elisabeth into the potting shed,
which smells of clover and good earth.
As her eyes adjust to the dimness, she sees
stacked clay pots, a watering can, a rusty spade,
and notebooks with covers that waffle from moist pages.
A photograph of Lise and Elisabeth at the river
is tacked to one wall. Their bare legs stretch
to the water, their straw hats tossed to the side.

The Peach-Colored House

Lise sets down a thin-stemmed glass
by linen napkins crisply folded into art.
Yellow tulips lean at elegant angles
this Sunday afternoon at Max Panck's house.
A little girl holds a felt doll as small as her thumb,
dressed in a red riding hood.
Her hooked arm holds a tiny straw basket.

Elisabeth talks with the girl, then joins Lise,
Max's son, Erwin, and Hildegard's husband, Paul,
who Lise seldom sees since he left KWI.
Paul says that the Jewish founder
of *The Science of Nature* was dismissed.
I agreed to replace him as senior editor. Not without guilt.

Better you than some Nazi, Erwin says.
The newspapers from Berlin are getting thinner.
And the government demands that only good news
about Germany cross our borders. Such as saying
Hitler has done away with poverty and crime.

No one will believe that, Lise says.

153

All they need is enough people to doubt
so they can forge ahead, Erwin replies.
Did my father tell you I quit my government job?
If they're going to fire Jewish employees,
then everyone should leave in protest.

Lise is touched by his words but says,
Perhaps you should keep working
for the government, do good from within.

That's what my father says. All his talk
about how laws are laws and must be obeyed,
even if wrong. Erwin grimaces.

What can one person do? Elisabeth asks.

Those words are like a flag waving the Nazis forward,
Paul says. *We who are less at risk must act.*
Every time one of us says, "I'd just lose my job
or reputation and for what?"
those in power know they can do anything.

Lise hears the little girl wail.
She can't find her Little Red Riding Hood doll.
Lise helps search through thickets of books,
silver spoons, crystal glasses, tulips,

frantic as a child lost in the woods.
A doll can't have just disappeared.

Singing

Wild geese return to the river.
Maybe German good sense is coming back
with the sweet-smelling lilacs
and linden trees' white blossoms.
Reports of new cruel laws fade that spring.
Lise is pleased that she didn't listen to those
who urged her to leave the country.
She's glad for wild strawberries, plums lined up
in market stalls, and students to teach.

Back at her desk, Lise reads papers from Paris
about how Irène and her husband and lab partner
Frédéric Joliot-Curie moved radioactivity
from one element to another. Lise tells Otto,
They claim to have created a new element
beyond uranium, expanding the periodic table.

It sounds like a stunt.
Perhaps an element called curiosum.

We should try to make new elements too.

I'm in the middle of other work. And Edith . . .
misses you. Will you come over for supper?

Walking to their house, Otto says,
Edith takes things hard.
I tell her we must look at the good.
Instead of the beggars who used to gather
by the park, I heard a group of boys singing!
I suppose wholesome lads like that were always
in the countryside, but not here in Berlin.

The Hitler Youth. Lise has seen boys
with close-cropped hair, khaki shorts and shirts,
black kerchiefs tied around the collars.
I hear some carry knives marked "blood and honor."

Don't believe everything you hear!
Otto shakes his head.
They just like to march and go camping.

The Old Green Hat

Lise studies papers about how Irène and Fred
pelted alpha particles at samples of elements
that weren't radioactive, then became so.
She also translates Enrico Fermi's reports
about how he cast neutrons instead of alpha particles
at atoms as they could be aimed
with more accuracy, force, and speed.
He and his team tested each element in the periodic table,
producing no radioactivity until reaching fluorine.
Then forty elements became radioactive.
Enrico believes he created a new element, number 93.

Lise describes this to Otto and Fritz. They agree
to try to make new elements. Lise sets out a plan.
They begin by replicating Enrico Fermi's experiments.
Otto and Fritz mix radium and beryllium powder.
It takes weeks to boil and extract enough
to fill a box the size meant to hold a ring.
They use this to make neutrons.
Lise and her assistants build equipment
to scatter the neutrons using gamma rays.
They aim for the nucleus, the smallest part
of a small atom, which isn't easy to strike.

If an invisible atom were as big as an eye,
the nucleus would be less than a speck within it.

Lise likes working with Otto every day again,
though he no longer wears the green hat, which is tattered.
They don't sing duets when something goes right.
Sometimes when she brings up current events,
he says, *I read the newspapers like any educated person,*
but I leave politics to the politicians.

Alone

In the laboratory, Lise and Otto discuss
puzzling results of experiments
and the new laws from Nuremberg.
Jewish children may no longer play
on seesaws or swings in the park.
Their mothers can't sit on the green benches,
but only those newly painted yellow.

The Reich now forbids Jewish scientists
from publishing papers or speaking at conferences.
Lise can't attend the Wednesday colloquiums.
She and Otto collaborate on papers
about their new experiments,
but publish the work as done by Otto Hahn.

It's the work that matters, Lise says.
But her throat tightens as if she might vanish.

Grateful

Lise hears footsteps pause outside the laboratory.
She opens the door and faces Kurt Hess.
His hair is shaved close on the sides,
while the top is left long and swept over his scalp.
He raises his arm with the swastika armband in salute.
Are you looking for something? Lise asks.
He moves down the hall rather than reply.

Lise goes back inside and tells Otto, *He's always
snooping around. They say he takes notes on us.*

*I don't care for fellows like him, but I suppose
it's natural to want to feel proud of our country.
We've lost some of that since the war.*

*Then we should take responsibility for a loss
of purpose, not blame Jewish thinkers
or say the old government was too liberal.*

*You sound like Edith. She reads
too much news and gets agitated.*

It's nice that she cares.

We all care, Lise. You know the pressure
I get to join the Nazi Party, and I will never.
He waves a letter. *I refused an invitation to lecture*
on our discoveries, telling them you're forbidden
from traveling now. I won't seem
to take credit for work we did together.

Lise's face heats up. *I'm sorry to sound*
ungrateful. You're a good friend.
A scientific reputation is minor
compared to some losses. Still,
she clings to it like a treasured ring
a refugee might sew into the lining of her coat.

Dusk

Leaving her apartment building, Lise opens
an umbrella and heads past Otto and Edith's house.
Seeing Edith standing in the rain,
she hurries over. *Are you locked out?*

I can't stay, but I don't know where to go.
Edith clutches her own arms.
Colors swirl around, then grab me.

Do the doctors help?

They give me medicine so the colors fade.
But I go away too, with the blues and reds.

Edith, let's get you back inside.

Edith shakes her head. *Maybe Otto was right.*
I shouldn't have encouraged
him to draw. I thought there would be more joy.
If something happens, you'll take care of him,
won't you? You're his godmother.

But Otto is his father!
And nothing will happen to you.

Nobody knows what will happen.
On my way to Wertheim's department store,
I heard screams coming from a basement.

Are you certain? Lise regrets her words
as soon as she speaks them. That question
has become as common as doubt. She says,
I'm sorry. Of course you heard what you heard.

What's Coming

Lise stands by the Geiger counter, listening
for a stuttering announcement of change.
A discovery that can be written in a sentence
may take years of working straight ahead,
alert for signs of when to detour.
She looks up as Otto enters and puts down
two packages. He always carries these
so he can shrug, with no spare arm to salute,
when he passes men wearing armbands with swastikas.

Edith had another rough night, he tells Lise.
She keeps saying, A great misfortune is coming.
She says she heard screams in the city.

Erwin told me that the police arrest
people they claim are enemies of the state.
Some are tortured in warehouses.

Quatsch. Nonsense. Such horrors can't happen
in a civilized country. Erwin is a nice enough chap,
but Max told me he's caught up with fanatics.

Erwin is an idealist. I like him.
Lise picks up the wastebasket to empty

in a bin behind the building, remembers
Anna's steady smile. She asks a secretary
for the address where Anna lives
with an aunt and writes a hopeful letter.

Sleepless

Lise brushes aside a moth with folded wings,
waiting for night. In bed, she hears
footsteps in the apartment overhead.
What does Kurt Hess watch and listen for?
Each creak in his floorboards, her ceiling,
makes her skin sting as if battered by pebbles.
She might be arrested for walking
into the wrong shop, asking the wrong question,
nothing, everything, being who she is meant to be.
Her body says, *Get out of this country.*

But her memory lilts with the voices
of friends urging her to stay.
She can't leave a laboratory that bears her name.

Unsaid

The laboratory wastebasket overflows.
The cloth-wrapped cake has long grown stale.
When Elisabeth enters at the end of the day,
Lise tells her, *I haven't seen Anna in a while.*

Do you think she's ill?

I don't know. Elisabeth, I'm tired.
I don't sleep much.
Sometimes I wonder if I belong here.

Of course you do. Things will change.
But I understand it's hard. I was warned
not to quote or name Jewish scientists.
If professors talk about relativity or how matter
equals energy, they must not say Einstein's name.

It's absurd to talk about electrons without referring
to James Franck or plant pigments such as chlorophyll
without mentioning Richard Willstätter.

But you must get some rest, Elisabeth says.
Do something that brings joy. My sister has tickets
to a concert she can't use. Will you come?

Stopping the Music

On the way to the concert hall, Lise and Elisabeth
pass police wearing black uniforms
and steel helmets as smooth as the heads of eagles,
visors curved down like beaks.
Leather gloves sharpen their hands like claws.

Lise and Elisabeth enter the lobby,
walk through a crowd of elegantly dressed people,
and take seats near the stage.
As Beethoven's symphony begins,
Elisabeth's chin bobs slightly with the rhythm.
In the midst of the music,
a man in a row ahead of them stands
and shoots up his arm in a Nazi salute.
People around him gasp.

The conductor pauses his own waving arms.
One by one, musicians lower
flutes, clarinets, and trombones.
The conductor turns and stares
at the man, who still salutes.
His voice is as commanding as a choir:
Sir, put down that arm.

The man takes back his seat.
The conductor again faces the musicians,
who start up where they left off.
No one in the audience stirs until the orchestra
reaches the beautiful end Beethoven intended.

After the applause, walking home, Lise says,
I'm grateful for people like that conductor.

He was brave, Elisabeth says.
But do such actions really do any good?

Something wrong happened and he said, Stop.
As long as people like me have sleepless nights
and others don't, nothing will change.

Address Unknown

In the bakery, the woman who's long greeted
Lise with, *Guten Tag, Frau Professor!* is silent
even when Lise asks, *How is your daughter?*
She plunks the cinnamon cake on paper
she fumbles instead of crisply folds.
When Lise says, *Danke,* the woman turns her back
rather than sending her off with a blessing.

Lise brings the cake wound in paper
without red-and-white twine to Elisabeth's apartment.
When she tells her about the silence,
Elisabeth says, *Maybe she was tired.*
Or if she meant to be rude, what makes you think
it's because you're Jewish? How would she know?

Saying a few kind words used to be easy.
Now being good is a feat.
I don't want cake from someone who hates me.

Nobody hates you. Maybe she's scared.
This is an upsetting time for everyone.

Is there a difference between hate and fear?
Lise has seen signs in cafés that say:

WE DO NOT SERVE JEWS. Some are propped behind
stacked dishes, half-hidden by owners who wish
they weren't ordered to show such signs.
Is there a line between people who follow rules
because they need to live and people who hate?

I'll go to the bakery the next time, Elisabeth says.

I want to buy my own cake! You can't help me,
Elisabeth. You with your study of race purity.
Lise's mouth wrenches, as if about to spit out
something sour. *Who do you think*
your friends in eugenics want to cleanse? Me.

We just want to end disease and distress.
Elisabeth's arms show patchy red marks left by bee stings.
Anyway, I can't just stop a line of study.
Some colleagues already call me disloyal
for saying agriculture didn't begin in Germany.

There's no point in calling ourselves
scientists if we don't tell the truth.

Are you telling me I should stop my work?
Resign from the genetics department?

I'm just asking you to think
about what your research might lead to.

You don't know what your atomic experiments will bring.

Lise spins around toward the door.
Elisabeth says. *You forgot the cake.*

I'd bring some to Anna, but she's gone.

What are you saying? Elisabeth stands still.
Are you suggesting the police took her away?

I don't know. They want us to get used to not knowing.
The letter Lise sent to Anna came back marked:
Return to sender. Gone east. Adresse unbekannt.

A Kind of Faith

Since Otto brought Edith to a sanatorium,
most nights he stays late at the laboratory.
When Lise asks about Hanno, Otto says,
At fourteen, he's just as happy to take bread
and sausage to his room for supper.

Both scientists find relief in work,
though the past three years have raised
more questions than answers.
They created substances that have characteristics
of elements with high atomic numbers.
Others aren't even radioactive.
What seemed fact collapses, bends back, billows,
turns again. *Could parts of a nucleus snap off?*
Lise asks. *I read a paper by Ida Noddack*
that suggests one might split.

She had not one shred of evidence! Otto scoffs.
Is that how they do chemistry in her part of the country?
Spouting moonshine with no proof?

Perhaps it's the way of what they call Aryan science.
Lise has heard Ida is friendly with Nazis.

It's time to work on something else, Otto says.

Not yet, Lise says. Science can grow
when people look past what they were told,
are willing to chase failures for hints
of what no one was looking for. *We're near the end.*

Otto makes a huffing sound. Of course
they don't know exactly what they're looking for
and can't know if they're near an end
or moving in the wrong direction.
Maybe her habit of hope
has ruined her judgment.

I haven't seen Elisabeth in a while.
Otto changes the subject.
He's used to her stopping by to ask
if Lise wants to join her for a walk or supper.
When Lise is silent, Otto glances at the full wastebasket.
Or Anna. Where has she been?

Lise shrugs. She's tired of questions
that can't be answered. But she won't leave this work,
won't give up her trust in a small beautiful ending.

Drops of Water

Lise gets on her black bicycle.
She pedals to Grunewald, called a forest
though it's more like a park. Ideas take their own time.
Work happens under trees as well as on tables.

Clouds thicken as she walks between trees.
Raindrops fall at one speed from the sky,
another from ferns. Some coast off birches
or curve through pine bark that's gnarled
where time and weather changed its course.
Molecules cling on each raindrop's surface,
pulling the water into the shape of a sphere.
Still that surface tension can be broken.
One drop becomes two. Every falling
drop holds a chance of change.

Train Tickets and Cake

Lise rides the train back from a niece's wedding
in Vienna. After the ceremony, Lise's sister Gusti
talked about how she misses Robert, how her husband
Justinian is painting, politics, and her new piano.
Now, as the train stops in Berlin, Lise sees
lines of people showing papers to guards.
Elisabeth steps past them, says, *I missed you.*

Lise understands she means for longer
than her trip to Vienna. There's more to say,
but first they make their way around people
being questioned before they're allowed to board a train.
Two guards lean over a mother, father, three children,
and two suitcases each held together with twine.
All look frightened except one girl.
Her soft, tilting body and steady smile
in a round face remind Lise of Anna.

One guard diligently inspects papers.
The other asks the children questions:
their names, simple arithmetic.
Lise and Elisabeth step closer as they ask
the smiling girl to do sums. She laughs.

A guard pushes her to the side,
waves on the parents and other children.

Elisabeth steps forward. *They're a family!*

Lise grabs her, hisses, *Stop!*
meaning, *What would I do without you?*

The mother rushes to sweep
her child toward her.
The father picks up the two suitcases
that might hold all they own,
turns from the train they will not board.

I should have believed you. Elisabeth chokes,
then sputters, *I was wrong to defend eugenics.*
It's not even science. You told me that. I'm sorry.

I miss Anna, Lise whispers.
I should have given her a whole cake.

You should have given her a train ticket out,
Elisabeth says. *You both should have gone.*

Sisters

In her laboratory Lise unfolds a newspaper and reads
about Nazi troops and tanks invading Austria.
A young man dashes down the hall, calls Lise
to the telephone, where an operator connects the sisters.
Thank goodness Robert is in Denmark, Gusti says.
Our own neighbors cheered for the Nazi soldiers
marching into the city. Church bells rang
as if it were a holiday. They draped flags with swastikas
from windows. People celebrated with sweet cream.

Lise thinks of her old passport, useless now
that German laws are Austria's laws, too.
She wishes she could tell Gusti to shelter
with her. But now neither one of them is safe.

What Matters

Lise mulls over contradictions,
what looks like error, but may be knots holding
shreds of truth if only they can be untangled.
What are they making? Much is not what it seems.

Lise heads to the center of Berlin to borrow a book
from a friend. She won't go to the library,
where signs prohibit Jewish readers
from sitting at tables.
A man on a bicycle swerves close.
Lise gasps, then sees it's Erwin,
his trousers tucked into his socks.
He steers his bicycle to the edge of the park.
Boys wearing khaki shirts and shorts
line up to hurl sticks at a goal.
They look about Hanno's age,
a thought marked with guilt or worry.
Lise hasn't seen her godson in months.

*Those Hitler Youth throw sticks the way
we thrust grenades during the war,* Erwin says.

Otto says they just like to sing and camp.

It starts that way, but they say Hitler is building
an army. Those boys are taught to look for signs
of political dissent. Some turn in their own parents.

Can it be that bad? Hitler is such an ignorant man.

People needn't be clever to destroy.
Lise, you should leave Germany.
It won't be easy. Now they forbid
distinguished people like you from going.
They're afraid professors will spread the truth
about crimes Nazis mean to hide from other countries.

What would my students think if I abandoned them?

They're starting to deport Communists, gypsies,
Jews, anyone who speaks against the Reich,
to concentration camps. People concentrated
in locked barracks against their will, Erwin says.
There's one at the old gunpowder factory in Dachau.
Lise, where would you go if you have a choice?

Lise remembers Eva's promise that Lise can count on her.
I have a friend in Sweden.
She thinks of James teaching in Chicago.
Hertha became the first woman physics professor
at Duke University. Her voice trembles. *America?*

Some universities in the United States were happy
to raise their status by hiring renowned physicists.
But most quotas of Jewish professors there
have been filled. What matters is to leave.

Elsewhere

After exercise class, Hildegard Rosbaud confides
her plans to go to England with her daughter.
Paul has wanted us to get out of Germany for a while,
but Angelika protested that she couldn't leave her friends.
That changed when she and other Jewish students
were told they couldn't come back to their school.

Won't Paul go too? Lise asks.

I'm the one who's Jewish, so Angelika is too.
Hildegard's eyebrows are penciled into perfect arches.
She smells of soap. *We need paperwork*
to show where we live, tax documents to show
how much money we have, a letter from a rabbi
and certificates from the police testifying
to my good character. A reference from our enemies!

They walk through the city, seeing people feed birds,
boys kneeling on the sidewalk shooting marbles.
Crows sweep over linden trees with heart-shaped leaves.
The friends stop at a building surrounded by winding lines
of people. Many stumble back down steps in tears.

Paul knows the director of the British Passport
Control Office, Hildegard says. Frank Foley
got Angelika and me visas to go to England.
The lines are so long because of his reputation
for stamping passports that legally shouldn't be stamped.
He knows people who will help travelers
without the proper papers cross borders.
Often parish priests, parsons of small churches.
And here in Berlin he knows who to bribe.

I should have left Germany sooner.
Now that it seems almost impossible
to get out, Lise knows she must. *Where will you go?*

I have a friend in England who wants to start a gym
and needs teachers. Paul always liked the British.
They put him in prison during the war, but when
the fighting ended, a guard gave him a bar of chocolate.
He wants me in a country ready to take a stand
against Hitler if there's a war. He says
they're already stocking gas masks in England.

Paper Lies

The government refuses Lise's request for a new passport.
The chief of police sends notice
that she is forbidden to leave Germany.

Lise meets with Hildegard by the river.
Maybe this is a sign I shouldn't go yet,
Lise says. *I want to finish a few more experiments.*

The risks are getting greater.
Hildegard shakes her head. *It may take a while,*
but Paul will arrange for papers that say
a new passport and visa are in process.
You must leave as soon as they're ready.
Niels Bohr is looking for somewhere you can go.

I can't use forged papers, Lise says.
I don't lie. Or break laws!

You will now, Liebe. Hildegard touches her wrist.
It might be the least of your worries.

Thorns

In the laboratory, Lise turns her head at the sound
of footsteps. She only truly trusts Otto, Fritz, his new wife,
Maria, a chemist, and Max von Laue,
whose teenaged daughter sometimes helps and learns here.
Hildy takes going to college for granted,
scarcely aware of a time when girls didn't have such chances.

Lise works harder than ever, hoping
to answer questions before she must leave the country.
But she's mystified. Instead of finding new elements
with atomic numbers past uranium,
Lise and Otto find signs of known elements
from the middle of the periodic table.

Stepping away can bring a new perspective.
She gets coffee and tells Otto,
I'm glad Edith is back from the sanatorium.

It's quite a nice place, really. Ladies
recline in chairs under blankets and read novels.
She had a new treatment that uses electricity.
She's getting better. Otto ends most
conversations about Edith this way.

He's scrupulous about the details of lab reports
but throws a cloak over disturbing behaviors.

On her way home, Lise sees Edith in her yard
clipping rosebushes. Few prune in midsummer.
Most wait till the blossoms have fallen.
She waves Lise over, says, *I need to talk
with you about Hanno. He wrote some foolish letters.*

Lise takes the clippers from Edith's trembling hands.
A boy who's fifteen is bound to bring worries,
but can't Edith see she has her own?
Her arms are scratched.
She needs gloves and sleeves.
Lise picks up a few roses from the grass,
hands some to Edith, and carries one home.

The Other Side of the Door

Lise sorts hundreds of photographs she took
of particles beaming toward the nuclei of atoms.
In science, much must be done over and over.
Needing to triple-check some results,
she walks upstairs to look for Otto.
By an office with an open door,
she overhears Kurt Hess say,
The Jewess endangers the institute.

Lise runs downstairs to her laboratory.
Otto follows more slowly. He says,
I'm sorry. The directors want you to resign.
It might be best if you don't come back.

Green Leaves

No one must suspect this night is different
from any other evening. Lise works late
writing about experiments with thorium,
careful with each digit and sign
that shape the forces of an equation,
invisible as the lift under birds' wings.

Lise runs a palm over paraffin blocks, lead vessels,
the equipment she designed: wires she strung,
knobs she tightened, tubing she measured.
She snaps down the green window shade.
A moth taps on the glass. No, that's footsteps.
Elisabeth quietly asks, *Can I help?*

Lise's arms stiffen. What does Elisabeth know?
Lise didn't tell her friend she was leaving Berlin.
Saying goodbye is dangerous. When police
ask where she's gone, it's safest if friends
have no secrets to confide or hide. Otto knows
and told Max she's going to visit her family.
On his desk calendar he wrote: *Lise goes to Vienna.*

I'm just finishing notes on our experiments.
Lise's voice cracks on the last word. Surely
Elisabeth isn't prying for weaknesses to report.
Lise can't ask her to water the geraniums.
But maybe when Elisabeth notices she's missing,
she'll come by to make sure the plants stay alive.

I tell my students about Jewish scientists.
Elisabeth speaks softly. *I say their names.*
I'm not brave, but if you have nightmares,
then so should I. She kisses Lise.
Her hair smells of leaves. *I'll be there*
cheering when you win that Nobel Prize.

If

Lise hangs her lab coat on its hook.
She pushes open the door with her elbow,
hears crickets as she crosses the street to her apartment.
Otto suggested she spend the night at his home.
If Kurt Hess or another Nazi hears she's fleeing,
surely the second place they'd look
is at the house of her longtime colleague.
Maybe Otto isn't thinking of danger from spies,
but danger from herself. He may fear she'll hide or bolt.

Lise rolls silk stockings, folds cotton dresses,
packs her hairbrush and ten marks, all the money
anyone is allowed to take from the country,
enough to live on for a few days if careful.
She must leave her good wool coat. If she's stopped,
her suitcase searched, she must look like a woman
on a summer excursion, not a scientist in exile.

She clicks the brass latches closed.
She can't bring her three green plates or the sewing box,
though she takes out an embroidery hoop, thread, needle,
and the scissors shaped like a bird to carry on the train.
She packs the little wooden duck Robert gave

her when she first left home, leaves behind
science notebooks and diagrams, diaries.
Thirty-one years of calling Berlin home.

The Corner

Lise is greeted by Otto and Edith, who repeats,
The great misfortune has happened.
Otto puts an arm around her thin shoulders.
Calm down. Everything will be all right.

Lise carries her suitcase to the spare room
but stops before the door to her godson's bedroom.
She remembers holding his small hand
when he was christened. She promised
she'd always look out for him.
She should have done better.

Hanno already has a bicycle, but Lise wants
to offer him hers. Maybe he'll lend it to a friend.
She'd like to know it's being used.
Lise knocks on the door. Hanno opens it.
His hair is shaved short on the sides, then swept
over his head. She sees crumpled brown shorts,
white knee socks, a black kerchief, a box of matches,
and a camping knife strewn in a corner.
No. No. No. Words gum to the back of her mouth.

The Gold Ring

In the morning, Otto says, *Hanno*
doesn't believe any of those things.
He just wants to be part of something.
Otto hands Lise a gold ring.
The ragged skin of his fingertips,
like hers, is reddened from radioactivity.
This was my mother's. In case you need it.
I'll keep on with the experiments and write
to you. I couldn't get far without your insights.
He looks out the window.
Paul Rosbaud will drive you to the station.
It's best no one sees you walking the wrong way.

The Falling Sky

Paul drives past buildings draped with red
and black banners branded with swastikas.
Dirk Coster and his family live in Holland now,
he says. *He talked to someone to get you
there past German border guards.*

Paul, please turn around. I can't go.
Lise grips the door handle.
The breezes through the car windows are hot.
*I'm sorry. I know you and Frank Foley
worked hard to get me papers.*
With lies that might save her life.
Max's son Erwin also helped.
And Niels Bohr found her a job
in a new nuclear physics institute in Stockholm.

Paul keeps driving straight ahead. He says,
*Chemistry changed much in the last war,
but if the wickedness here leads to another war,
physics may be crucial. Articles submitted to our magazine
sometimes suggest tactics for making weapons.
I may send you some articles to pass along
to Hildegard or other friends in England.*

Paul's words blur like traffic coming from all directions.
When he stops the automobile, wishes her luck,
Lise steps out and heads toward the train platform.
Troopers with straight backs check identifications.
One guard's eyes shift to the side, then to her face.
Is he daring her to let go of the scream inside her?

When he asks her name, she says,
Frau Professor Meitner.
She reads in his slumped shoulders
the bored assumption that she's a professor's wife.

Lise takes a seat among women who tilt
knitting needles or open books,
but forget to count stitches or turn pages.
No one swaps magazines.
Children don't bounce on the seats.
Lise takes out the old embroidery hoop
to look like someone who cares only about shades
of red. What did Dirk do to forge a promise
that she could get past Germany's border?
Could he have spoken with someone corrupt?

Metal wheels scrape on metal tracks.
Edith's words clatter inside her:
I must talk to you about Hanno.
Will that boy turn her in?

Crossing

The train screams to a stop in midafternoon.
Peddlers pass hot broth and sausages
through windows, open their palms for coins.
Some men, women, and children get on at the station.
Others are pulled off, crying, pleading, protesting.

Passkontrolle. The voice of the Nazi officer
who stops beside Lise is clipped, dangerously ordinary.
He slowly turns the passport pages,
studying each one as if it could save or convict her.
Lise feels the hard stamp of eyes on her.
She struggles to appear like a traveler
with perhaps a cup of tea on her mind,
hides the woman who aches to scream,
bolt from the train, and run for her life.
Should she offer the gold ring that burns into her hand?

At last he nods and returns her papers.
Maybe he's tired. Maybe he's kind
or hates the job he took, seeing no other
means to put food on his family's table.
Maybe her eyes remind him of his mother's.

The Lost Sea

The locomotive's smoke thickens.
The brakes catch. The world becomes quiet.
Lise makes her way to the door,
where a Dutch guard steps past a German officer
exactly as Dirk arranged.
The guard fumbles through Lise's papers.
Feeling sick from relief and the lies that saved her,
she steps out onto Holland's good green ground.
Dirk and his wife welcome her with a safe roof,
potato soup, fresh bread and butter
around the table with their four children.

Later, Lise takes another train,
boards a ferry to another free country.
She tastes salt in the air.
Men fling nets from fishing boats.
The sea's wrinkles and folds catch light.
She grabs the rail, frightened as Noah's family
must have been for forty days and nights,
uncertain if they'd ever reach a safe shore.

Harbor

Houses with red-framed windows are shuffled
within cliffs. Sunlight turns yellow bricks golden.
Bells chime from Stockholm's city hall
over a statue of a man struggling
to stay on a rearing horse.

Eva hugs her, asks her to come
with her to the countryside in the north.
I'm so glad to see you, Lise says.
But please, will you find me a hotel room?
She hates to say goodbye to the one person
she knows in Sweden, but she can't board
another train. She must stay in the city
where she has work and can get mail quickly.

I don't teach in the summer. Eva's hair
and short eyelashes are now more gray than brown.
I'll go book two rooms and stay a while,
help you get used to speaking Swedish.

Lise waits on a park bench that's not painted
yellow, where anyone may sit.
Boats tug on ropes by the pier.

Blue flags with gold crosses wave in the wind.
She's a person between places, not knowing
if she can ever go—where? Even language is broken.
She replaces the word *home* with *back to Berlin*.

The Weight

Lise is safer in Stockholm than in Berlin,
but it's hard to feel she belongs
while trying to sleep in a hotel room
with pictures of places she's never been.
Or working in the new research institute
where there's little equipment and few scientists.
None care to hear from a foreigner and a woman.

This land caught her from a fall,
but gratitude is a pulse, not solid ground.
Each day feels heavy as an old winter coat,
thrust upon her without asking if it fit.
She looks through a window at the fog,
writes letters to Otto about their experiments.

Two Sides of the Medal

Niels invited Otto to the physics institute to speak
about their work, giving Lise a chance to see him.
She takes a train and a ferry to Copenhagen,
happily looks over the water at narrow houses
the colors of cherries, lemons, and green apples.

But even in Denmark, it's safest for Lise and
Otto to keep their names more than a breath apart.
While Otto lectures in an auditorium, Lise waits
with Hilde Levi at the home of Niels and Margrethe.
Lise looks over the bookshelves,
picks up Niels's Nobel gold medal.
On one side is the engraved profile of benefactor
and scientist Alfred Nobel. On the other, two women
rise from clouds with tunics falling to their waists:
the Spirit of Science lifts a veil off Mother Nature.
Sometimes Nature decides when the veil should go.

They hear footsteps. Lise hugs Niels, Margrethe,
and Robert. She sits by Otto, who reports
that Fritz and Maria had a healthy baby boy.
Edith is back resting in a sanatorium.

I'm sorry. Lise reaches into her purse.
I brought back your ring.

Otto shakes his head. *Perhaps it may still be of use.*
Elisabeth was shocked to find your apartment,
without you. She collected a few things.
Some green plates she said you like. She couldn't take
much, nothing the police would notice as missing.

Lise is silent, imagining her rooms being ransacked.
Niels says, *Everyone was intrigued by Otto's talk*
about your search for elements beyond uranium.

Lise's friends discuss the baffling results.
She walks to the window, looks through
the dark glass. She sees her reflection, some split
sunflower seeds on the sill, the tracks of birds.
Long ago Eva told her some of their names
in Swedish, but she doesn't remember. Fine.
Let birds be red or black or speckled.
Names can help one see or get in the way.

The Night of Broken Glass

The library shelves at the new institute
are still empty, but a globe sits on a table.
Lise trails her fingertips over borderlines
that have changed since the mapmaker chose colors.
She rereads Gusti's letter from Vienna,
where shattered glass filled streets
after Nazi mobs hurled rocks through windows.
Nazi police arrested thousands,
including her husband and their brother Walter.
They were shoved into trains, taken, we're told,
to an old gunpowder factory in Dachau.
Lise, I don't know if we'll ever see them again.

Crystal Chandeliers

The dark sky is pierced by the spires of city hall.
Wagons loaded with coffee urns, crates of oranges,
and bottles of champagne rattle
over slush-covered cobblestones.
Lise is glad for the wool coat Eva sent her.
She wears it over her good dress to the grand party
celebrating Enrico Fermi's win of a Nobel Prize.

Under chandeliers, women in gowns and diamonds
mingle with men in starched white shirts
and bow ties, black suit coats with tails.
Lise greets Laura Fermi, who she's met
at conferences where they've spoken in French,
which Lise finds easier than Italian. She says,
I see your husband is busy shaking hands.
If I don't get a chance to congratulate him tonight,
please pass it on and thank him
for including my name and Otto's in his speech.

It will be your time next for the Nobel Prize.

We're still puzzled by some of our results.

Enrico had doubts too. Did they really find
elements 93 and 94, and you and Otto 95 and 96?
Science isn't quick or clear, but Mussolini insisted
Enrico call his discovery certain. Anyway,
it was good of you to come so far to pay your respects.

I live here now. Berlin is no longer safe for me.

You're Jewish? Laura takes a quick breath,
looks around the gleaming hall. *So am I.*
In Rome such things used to not matter.
Italy changed when Mussolini and Hitler became friends.
We're raising our children as Catholic.
God is all the same to the young. But we don't like them
growing up in a country run by gangsters.

Will you leave Italy? Lise asks.

It's forbidden. It took effort just to come here
for the prize. Luckily, Mussolini craved the chance
to claim that Italy's scientific glory has returned.
Laura lowers her voice. *My father was an admiral*
in the Great War, which they'll respect, we think.
But could we leave him? I lived my whole life in Rome
amid fountains and lemon trees. It's so cold here.
I had to find leggings for the children.

It's not cold all the time, Lise says, though
she's never felt warm here. Should she urge Laura
to leave her homeland before it's too late?
She wonders if she, too, looks lost.

Snow

Just before Christmas, Lise takes a train to an inn
near the cottage where Eva and her husband live.
Robert books a room by hers. He says, *I wanted
to see my mother, but she insisted Vienna is too dangerous.*

*She's right. I'm trying to arrange for her to come here.
She won't leave until your father gets back
from Dachau.* Lise's voice cracks
with the effort to hope that will happen.
What took me so long to leave Germany?

You had work you love, Robert says.

And I still do. She's relieved to change the subject.
*I get letters from Otto, who peppered neutrons
at uranium. Rather than create the next higher element,
barium appeared in the beaker.*

That's chemically absurd. Did he examine for impurities?

*Otto and Fritz's work is impeccable.
They checked the instruments and math many times.*

One or two of the ninety-two protons in the nucleus of uranium
might split off, but not dozens, changing to barium.

Tante Lise, I came here to ski.

I can walk as fast as you can ski.
Lise stuffs Otto's letter in her coat pocket.
Robert straps on his wooden skis and glides.
Lise strides through the snow.
As she swings up her arms, her belly stretches.
She brushes snowflakes off her sleeve, remembers
Niels comparing an atom's nucleus to a drop of water,
held together by surface tension.

Could a nucleus struck by particles wobble,
then thin in the middle like pulled taffy
or a small boy's belly when an aunt
grabs his hands to spin him around?
Breaking at a weakened middle,
the two new nuclei could create energy once held in mass,
which Einstein said can't just disappear.

Lise sweeps snow off a fallen tree trunk to sit.
She takes off her mittens, reaches into her pocket
for the warm stub of a pencil she brought from Berlin.
She writes on the back of Otto's letter,

calculating how the mass of the two nuclei
would equal the energy created as they repelled each other.
They'd make about two hundred million electron volts of energy.

Lise looks across the white field, the wide sky.
Maybe the scent of pine, the pinch of cold
in a country that still feels foreign helps her see
past old answers to what once seemed impossible.
She understands that when Otto pelted uranium
with particles, the nucleus shattered, releasing vast energy.

The setting sun slants light across snow
that briefly glimmers pink and blue.
Lise crumples the paper in her pocket.
With Robert skiing beside her,
Lise finds her old footprints,
hurries to get back to the inn before dark.

Disappearing

Eva and Niklas serve Christmas dinner by a tree
decorated with tinsel, angels, and flickering candles.
When the conversation turns to politics,
Robert pushes away the codfish and potatoes.
They're too salty. He sits at the piano,
holds notes that stir wonder just beyond grasp.

Lise goes back to Stockholm, where she writes
her interpretation of the experiments. She sends
this to Otto with an explanation of how uranium split
into barium, element 56, and krypton, element 36,
their atomic numbers adding to that of uranium, number 92.

Robert runs experiments back in Copenhagen,
where he has better equipment than she has.
Scattering uranium neutrons in an ionization chamber
shows waving lines rather than pale dots.
Proof of what they'll call nuclear fission.
Otto and Fritz also repeat experiments
that show that their team,
Enrico Fermi and his co-workers,
and Irène and Frédéric Joliot-Curie
all along were splitting atoms,
finding not new elements as they thought,

but the fallout of small nuclear explosions.
They all overlooked what no one believed could happen.

Otto writes to thank Lise for her insights.
I'll publish the results but won't mention your name.
As you know, my job is vulnerable now.

Lise knows it's safest that their names not be linked.
The Nazis likely suspect Otto of hiding
information about the disappearance
of his longtime science partner.
But her hands are cold as she boils water for tea.

An Old Song

Lise's sister and her husband enter
the apartment she found to share with them.
Justinian is thin, fragile, with bruises on his wrists.
He stares ahead, silent as Lise and Gusti talk
about their brother Walter. After he was released
from Dachau, he and his wife joined
a sister and her husband who fled to England.
Others in their family seek work in the United States.

Gusti tells her about the night
when Justinian and thousands of men were arrested.
Troopers barged into our home.
They stamped seals on furniture to be taken.
Justinian's desk. They tore pages from his books.
One man swung a poker on the piano keys.
I suppose they didn't think they could get it down the stairs.

Lise imagines the piano keys cracking like bones.
She lets out her breath, thankful
the poker didn't land on her sister's hands.
Oh, my Liebe. You'll play again.

I was ordered outside with other women
to sweep up glass from the broken windows.
We stepped through scum and blood and ashes.
Gusti turns as Justinian hums the old song
they once sang with Robert:
One yellow duck, two, three yellow ducks!

Gusti whispers, In Dachau, the guards played
children's songs on a phonograph.
To cover screams of people being tortured.

Land and Sea

A letter from Elisabeth says she's been reprimanded
for *political unreliability.*
I'm afraid they'll take away my teaching credentials.
Students reported that she spoke of Jewish scientists,
glossed over sections in *Introduction to Genetics,*
and wrote letters protesting state policies.

Lise puts away the letter. She knows Elisabeth
wants sympathy, but it's not in her now to give.
Lise helps make plans for Gusti and Justinian to sail
to England just before the Nazi army invades Poland.
In response to that hostility, France and England declare war
on Germany. Soon the Nazis capture Holland.
In Paris, German soldiers march under the Arc de Triomphe,
drape banners with swastikas from the Eiffel Tower.

Lise visits Copenhagen to work with Robert.
She sees Niels, back from New York, where he looked
for jobs for scientists trying to escape Germany.
And I saw Enrico. He used the Nobel Prize money
to board a ship to America with Laura and their children.
Niels's wiry hair is brushed back,
his eyebrows a slash across his long face.

I talked with him, Leo, and Einstein
about the experiment you interpreted.
They all said, We should have seen that!
Once one person names something,
it can be simple for others to see too.

And Leo is working out how nuclear fission
could start a chain reaction.
Releasing two neutrons that become four.
Those four reactions set off eight. Those explode
to sixteen and so on, making enormous power.

Lise feels the weight of these words in her bones.
What she, Robert, Otto, and Fritz found
is no longer theirs. She wonders what it will become.

Butter and Gold

Every month or two Lise rides a train, then a ferry,
to Copenhagen to use the institute's good equipment.
She says goodbye to Robert as he leaves
for a job in England he's secretive about.
One morning while walking, Lise hears
the sputter and roar of German airplanes.
Papers skitter from the sky.
She picks up a leaflet, reads the misspelled Danish:
Accept the protection of the German Reich.

Gulls caw. Clogs clap on cobblestones.
Lise walks past soldiers at the post office,
the police station, and the newspaper building.
These Nazis don't march with the snap of those in Berlin.
Their faces don't stay quite as tight as a mask.
But any one might grab her arm, end her life.

Back at the institute, Lise asks Niels,
Won't Denmark fight back?

*Our army is small. Resisting would mean
a massacre,* he says. *German soldiers may walk*

217

on our streets now, but we're told
the country will go on mostly as usual.

Niels, anyone even partly Jewish is in danger.
You and Margrethe should leave.
And Hilde, and George and his wife.

I founded this institute. I love this country.
Niels looks at the garden where his grandchildren play tag.
The Nazis mostly want Denmark's butter and bacon.
We can give that if it means keeping our freedom.
We'll take precautions. Let's get to the laboratory.

Margrethe, Hilde Levi, and George's wife, Pia,
burn newspaper clippings, letters, and lists
of people Niels helped escape from Germany.
Margrethe gathers three Nobel Prize medals.
What should we do with these? James left
his here when offered a chance to teach in the United States.
His luggage would have been searched before he got on a ship.
He could have been arrested for taking gold from Germany.

Lise picks up a medal engraved with the name
of Max von Laue. *Like Otto, Max refused to join*
the Nazi Party and protests their policies.

James is safe across the sea, Niels says. *But if
the Nazis found this one, they might throw Max in prison.*

I can dissolve the gold so it looks like any old liquid.
George tightens his face as he mixes nitric acid
with hydrochloric acid in a one-to-three ratio.
The medals hiss as they becomes part
of a dusty yellow-orange solution.
We'll stash this among other bottles in the closet,
George says. *Once the world is safe again,
we can turn it back into gold.*

It's always good to have a chemist around.
Niels affectionately slaps his friend's arm.

A New Calling

In the summer, Lise picks wildflowers
she puts in a jar by a stack of stationery.
She writes to Otto, Elisabeth, and Max von Laue,
who sends back news from Berlin. So does his daughter,
Hildy, who now works at the old pine tables at KWI,
wearing the lab coat Lise left on its hook.

Lise brushes off pollen that drifts to the table,
writes letters to help relatives, friends,
and strangers escape to safe places.
The city hall bells clang every quarter hour.
In winter, the silver radiator hisses and clanks.
It takes seventy letters to get physicist
Hedwig Kohn to Stockholm. She stays
with Lise until women's and Jewish organizations
arrange for her to teach in the United States.

Paul Rosbaud sends Lise coded versions of articles
submitted to his magazine that hint of plans
for tanks, submarines, guns, and explosives.
To help the Allies' war effort,
Lise sends on some coded articles to Paul's wife.
Hildegard passes them on to British military men.

Lise also transfers mail sent from Paul to Frank Foley.
After British citizens were ousted from Berlin,
Frank set up a passport office in Stockholm
that does more than process passports.
Frank gives Lise scientific articles to bring to Niels,
often with lightly marked words.
Niels shows Lise messages shrunk on microfilm.
These were wrapped in foil, then tucked
in a spy's false tooth, to be read with a microscope.
He says, *Soon we may be called*
to do more than pass along messages.

Shelter

Lise opens her apartment door, stunned
to see Niels, his clothes and hair damp.
When he's safely inside,
he tells of crossing the sea to Sweden,
hiding among herring boxes stacked on the deck.
We got word that the Nazis planned
to arrest all the Jewish citizens of Denmark.
Freight ships near the sound are at the ready
to be filled, then head to concentration camps.
Now Jews are hiding in sheds, warehouses, cottages,
barns, basements, and church lofts.
But they can't stay in those places forever.
At the start of the war, the king of Sweden
promised asylum here. With this new threat,
he should remind my countrymen and -women
they're safe here. I'll visit the king.
Niels runs his hand down his long face.
Then you and I must talk. I was asked to deliver
a message for you from scientists in America.

That evening, after Niels returns from the palace,
they meet at the home of friends.
They lean toward the radio, listening to King Gustav V

tell those in hiding, *You are welcome here.*
The radio keeps playing the king's words
so they can be heard across the sea.

Lise looks out the window, though
she can't see the shore where fishermen
may be setting aside nets,
steering their boats through the dark.
She imagines sails unfurled,
ropes scraping, oars splashing
as fishermen call out like Noah, *Come, hurry.*
Now there is not a single ark, but
rowboats, barges, vessels with room for all.

Invitation

The next morning Niels tells Lise that his wife
should be on her way across the strait
in a boat with their children, grandchildren,
George, Pia, and Hilde. *I wish I could see them settle here,*
but the Nazis are on alert, knowing Jews are fleeing.
The British warned they're especially after me,
so they arranged a small plane to get me to England.

I'll make sure Margrethe and the others
have safe places to stay, Lise says.

Thank you. I'll go from England to America.
Those countries want your help too.
They're using your discovery of nuclear fission
to work on an atomic bomb.

I wanted to learn about atoms, not make a weapon!
Lise knows he's not speaking of the bombs
now dropped by planes, smashing
and burning whatever is beneath.
The explosion from splitting atoms
could damage the air for miles,
burn down neighborhoods, kill children

and householders just going about their days.
The terrible possibility turns Lise's hands cold.

Fortunately, most of Germany's best physicists,
like you and Einstein, have left, Niels says.
But spies suggest they're trying to build a bomb.
The allied nations must build one first.
James, Enrico, Leo, and others are working
in New York, Chicago, and now Los Alamos.
I was asked to go there to advise.
They hired Robert. They want you to come
to the laboratory in New Mexico too.

To help make a bomb?
Niels, we are scientists, not warriors!

An atomic bomb could end the war sooner,
saving lives. I hope it won't have to be used,
but we must be prepared. The Nazis must be stopped.
Lise, you've heard about the disappearances
of people who didn't escape Germany's borders.

Yes. Lise squeezes her eyes shut.
She turns her mind to a laboratory
filled with fine equipment. She imagines
working with James Franck and Leo Szilard,

who would be quick to understand
that one exploding nucleus could split another
nearby, setting off a chain reaction.
She could work with Robert, whom she's loved
since he was small and gave her a wooden duck
so she wouldn't be lonely in Germany.
Now he's a respected physicist,
and furious that his father was tortured
when imprisoned in the Dachau camp.

Lise is furious too. But she remembers
the screams of injured soldiers when she worked
taking X-rays during the last war. She remembers
men blinded or missing arms, parts of faces gone,
and claims that terrible weapons would stop the war sooner.

Please tell the Americans I won't work with them.
Lise discovered what she discovered.
She can't stop how nuclear fission is used,
but she doesn't have to help, and she won't.
With all that's been taken, she holds on to her belief
that a single person speaking a single word
can change the shape of what comes next.
No, she says again. *I will have nothing to do with a bomb.*

Yellow Tulips

After Max Planck gives a lecture in Stockholm,
he invites Lise to dinner at a restaurant.
A cloth covers the table holding a vase of tulips
the color of bees or a child's drawing of the sun.
After some talk of science and Berlin,
Max says, *I worry about Erwin.*
So does his wife. She says he's rarely home.

He helped me escape from Berlin. I'll always
be grateful. Unjust laws must be broken.

Max nods. *I don't travel much anymore.*
I used to love to visit other countries.
I was proud of where I came from.
But we have done terrible things in Germany.
Terrible things must happen to us.

Lise takes the wrinkled hand of a man
who resisted wrongs the best way
he knew how. And still takes responsibility,
saying *we* when he could have said *they*.

But the ark of science never sank, Max says.

Instead it sailed past Germany's borders
with Albert Einstein, James Franck, Leo Szilard,
Hertha Sponer. With your nephew Robert. With you.

More Smoke

Mail, newspapers, and radio shape Lise's days.
She learns that bombs were dropped over Berlin.
Smoke twisted over smashed bridges, split cherry trees,
and crumpled bicycles by the Kaiser Wilhelm Institute.
The roof caved in. Windows blew out.
The pine table with paraffin blocks, prisms,
and pencils turned to ashes and smoke.
Max's peach-colored house also went up in flames.
The rosebushes, green wicker chairs,
and bookshelves all turned to rubble.
Was the Little Red Riding Hood doll ever found?

Later, Lise learns that a briefcase exploded
in Hitler's meeting room.
The Nazis accuse many of treason,
including Max's son. Erwin Planck was hanged
in a prison where eight iron hooks
looped with piano wire were fastened to a wall.

All the Names

Shortly before Germany surrenders,
Hitler kills himself. While the war continues
with Japan, Lise writes letters trying to learn
which old friends are still alive.
Her hands feel pinched with grief and guilt
to have escaped as she reads of innocents
who died without prayers, stories, gravestones.

White buses painted with red crosses
leave Sweden by ferry. Rescuers drive them
across Germany to concentration camps
in Dachau, Bergen-Belsen, Theresienstadt.
They bring back starving, wounded people.
Some are cared for by Danish nurses and doctors
who escaped to Sweden on fishing boats.

Courageous people drove those white buses.
Heroes sailed or rowed boats, rescuing thousands.
Still, in the crime and misery that flooded Europe,
millions died. Still more mourn and remember.
Lise hopes Noah and his wife—what *was* her name?—
didn't just blink at the rainbow and get on with their lives.
She hopes they left the battered ark standing
on the new shore as a reminder of what was lost.

News of the World

Lise rents a cottage in a village near Eva's home.
She hikes, swims, wrangles with memory and forgetting.
One afternoon she changes the radio station
from violins' low lingering
to trumpets' and clarinets' rowdy rhythms.
She hunts for a coin for the farmer who promised
to bring by a basket of eggs and a pint of goat milk.
The music is broken by an announcement
that an atomic bomb was dropped
over the Japanese city of Hiroshima.
Before they could even fall
wild geese   sparrows   moths
turned into sky and smoke.
Over the radio, the United States president speaks
of the size, secrecy, and cost of his country's mission.
As he describes nuclear fission and praises
the scientists behind the work, Lise unlatches
the door. She runs through a field into the woods,
bent under the weight of imagining the sky
over Japan breaking into blazes.

Maybe a boy steered a bicycle.
Maybe a baby played peekaboo.

A girl chased a frog by a rice field.
Another made a leaf-crown. Gone.

A woman adjusted the focus of a microscope.
Men tossed fishing nets into a river. Gone.
Old people might have rubbed sore knees,
thumbed through newspapers
for weather forecasts as smoke
waved like water over newly black earth.

At last Lise crosses the meadow back to the cottage.
The farmer stiffly holds her egg basket
as she stands near reporters who rush toward Lise.
We heard you invented the atomic bomb!
Lise steps past the farmer toward the door.
A reporter snaps their picture.

Edges of Words

The next morning Lise sees the photograph
in the Stockholm *Expressen* with the caption:
Scientists discuss nuclear secrets.
The *New York Times* reports that the crucial
component to constructing a bomb was brought
to America by a Jewish female physicist.
Other newspapers carry the distorted story shaped
from Albert Einstein's and Niels Bohr's reports
that Lise Meitner unraveled the mystery of nuclear fission.
They write as if there's a straight line between
discovering a phenomenon and inventing a weapon.
She hates being praised for what she didn't do,
and never wanted to do.
Newspapers report American soldiers
cheering with hope that they can go home soon,
though Japan hasn't yet surrendered.
Lise can think only about the people who died,
cruelly, as perhaps she more than most can imagine.

Three days after the atomic bomb exploded
over Hiroshima, a neighbor with a telephone runs over
to fetch Lise. There's a call from America.
Lise is asked to speak with the former First Lady,
a recent widow, now working to form the United Nations.

Lise hopes for a chance to explain
that while she found secrets of nuclear fission,
she never worked on an atomic bomb.

The telephone operator connects her to NBC broadcasters.
Eleanor Roosevelt says, *You are another Marie Curie.*
Perhaps we women can work together
to find ways to create a lasting peace.

Yes, Lise vows to work for an end to wars!
But everyone must look back before we can see
a way ahead and say, I'm sorry.

That day, while Lise thinks of what else
she should have said, an American plane
drops another bomb, this time over the city of Nagasaki.
A Japanese woman slipped off her sandals
by the steps, peeled a mandarin orange,
and worked out an equation. A boy drew a cat.
Bells gonged from a temple before it toppled.
Shreds and scraps of paper with edges of words flutter.
A red bird flies over a nest for the last time.

Another Country

Stars sparkle in the wide sky over the Atlantic.
Lise stands on the deck, heading toward America.
Before boarding the ship, she spent some time
in England visiting Walter and his wife,
Gusti and Justinian, who are proud of Robert's
secretive, important work in New Mexico.

The ship docks in New York. Lise heads
down the ramp into a crowd of strangers.
A dark-haired young man waves. Robert says,
I drove across the country. I wanted to surprise you.

You grew a beard!

I became a British citizen before
I came here, and wanted to look the part.
While waiting for her luggage, enough clothing
and books for six months, they find a secluded spot.
Robert tells her of his present work at Los Alamos.
We want to focus on the good that atomic power can bring.

Now that you've shown what it can destroy.

235

If we hadn't dropped the bomb, many more
thousands of American and Japanese soldiers
might be dead or maybe even still fighting.

Lise grabs his arm as reporters head toward them.
Robert, get me out of here.

Tante Lise, people here lost sons, brothers,
and husbands in the war trying to save Jewish people.
They see you as someone who makes their sacrifices worthwhile.
Reporters will ask what you think of Beethoven
and Mickey Mouse. Just smile and say something nice.

Truth

Lise's sister Frida, who teaches math at a college
in New York, takes her shopping
for a black velvet gown. Lise wears it
to a Women's National Press Club gala,
where she's honored as Woman of the Year.
She meets nine other notable women, including
an artist who paints flowers larger than life
and a choreographer for Broadway musicals.
Lise sits amid ferns and flags
beside President Truman, who says,
So you're the little lady who got us into this mess.
Lise shakes her head, tries to explain,
but the president smiles and changes the subject.

The *Saturday Evening Post* reports that a few years back
Lise snuck out of Germany with a bomb
in her handbag that she smuggled to the Allies.
Strangers who saw her photograph stop her in diners
or when boarding taxis, asking for her autograph.
Lise takes the train to Washington, DC, to visit another sister
whose husband teaches at the Catholic University of America,
where Lise will be a visiting professor for a semester.
She lectures with chalk on the cuffs of her sleeves,
looking out at students' hopeful faces.

In the evenings she tends to stacks of letters asking her
to speak to Girl Scout troops, join an aviation board,
help five thousand Jewish refugees find new homes
or a man with cancer pay for radiation treatments.

A producer from Metro-Goldwyn-Mayer tells her
of a movie they're making called
The Beginning or the End. MGM wants to use
the name of the Woman of the Year, cast as the girl
who knew the world's most terrifying secret.
Lise reads the script, which features a woman like her,
presumably younger and more glamorous,
who tucks away directions for a bomb
and heads into dark Berlin streets. She's followed
by a handsome assistant who's gunned down
by Nazis while she escapes with papers she sends to Einstein.

When Lise declines the use of her name,
MGM offers more money. Lise objects to her portrait,
but still more to how the writer shaped the script
as a thrilling military success story.
She couldn't keep the atomic bomb from being built.
She can't even stop a movie that glorifies
death and destruction from being made.
But she can refuse to let her name be used.
No, nein. She holds fast to truth.

She won't wish that she didn't discover
what she discovered. But she wishes everyone
would try to see as if by the light of two candles:
one calling to witness, one to remember.

Humanitarians

Lise speaks before congresswomen and members
of the American Association of University Women.
She receives honorary degrees from Smith College
and Brown, Purdue, and Rutgers Universities.
At Harvard and MIT, Lise talks about atomic theory
and science as a path toward truth and wonder.

After Lise lectures at Princeton University,
she asks to tour the physics building
but is told women aren't allowed inside.
She has dinner with Albert Einstein,
whose wiry hair has turned silver.
He tells her that soon after her discovery,
Leo persuaded him to sign a letter to the president,
urging that America build an atomic bomb
before the Nazis did. *Far into the war we realized*
the Germans might not have one.
Then James wrote a letter signed by many scientists
who worked to build the bomb pleading
that it be demonstrated far from people.
Einstein's brown eyes darken.
The president didn't want our opinions.

Some say it's fortunate the interpretation
escaped me when I was still in Germany, Lise says.
We don't know if the Nazis tried to build a bomb,
but it's lucky they didn't get a head start.

For those who believe in luck. God doesn't play dice.
Urging the president to build a bomb
was the greatest mistake of my life.
Now I'm helping form a group to promote peace.
Einstein bows his head, then looks straight at her.
Many brilliant scientists were asked to help
build an atomic weapon. Lise, you did the right thing.
I'm glad that one humanitarian said no.

The Memory of Songs

After speaking to students at Duke University,
Lise spends the evening with Hertha Sponer,
who tells her she plans to marry James Franck.
He's been lonely since his wife died.
But he'll keep his job at the University of Chicago
and I'll stay here. When I was hired ten years ago,
the president of Caltech wrote here saying
a woman professor would damage
the physics department's reputation.

I'm glad they chose the person most qualified.

But to make sure no one complains,
I look after more than my share of students
and publish plenty of research.

Will you ever go back to Berlin?

My sister tried to save people. We believe
she was murdered in a concentration camp.
After Lise expresses her sorrow, Hertha says,
I'm proud of her and other family I want to see
someday. Will you go back? How is Elisabeth?

I don't know. Lise would like to hold a hand again.
I miss the way Otto and I sang when we got something right.

You got a lot right.

The next day Lise is given a letter from Edith
with postmarks showing it had followed her about.
Lise reads quickly, her breath pumping: No. *No.*
For years she and Otto heard their names
spoken together as nominees for a Nobel Prize.
But it seems the prize will go to just one.

Hands

Otto is pulled away by reporters in Stockholm.
Lise watches his back as Edith asks Lise to help her
find a gown to wear to the ceremony. *And I want*
to buy shoes, sugar, sausage, and coffee to send
back to Berlin, where most shops are empty.
We can catch up. But no talking about politics!

They spend a morning going in and out of stores
before sitting down for coffee. Edith says, *You know*
it's not Otto's fault the prize was given just to him.

Yes, the Nobel committee makes the decision.
Lise's colleagues say committee members noted
she hadn't published in scientific journals these past years.
Surely they knew that was forbidden
to someone called an enemy of the German state.
She recently counted all the times she was nominated:
Twenty-eight, often along with Otto.
The committee well knew her name and work.

She takes a breath, asks, *How is Hanno?*

Edith's eyes brim with tears, as if
she knows the cost to Lise to ask about her son.
Edith shows her a picture of Hanno,
his German army uniform sleeve folded
and pinned over his missing left arm.

He was a lieutenant. He won two Iron Crosses.
Edith reaches into her purse, takes out a badge
embossed with an eagle: sharp beak and claws,
back straight as the lines of the sword,
and a swastika the bird uses as a perch.
Hanno married the nurse who cared
for him when they amputated his arm.
I'm sorry you missed their wedding.

I missed many things.

These young men didn't really have a choice.
I'm so ashamed. Edith bends over, chokes.
Lise takes her hand. Edith's palm shows pricks of blood
where she clutched the badge too hard.
Lise remembers Hanno as a baby,
uncurling his small fingers, five now gone.
She supposes he won't be an artist now.
She peels off the badge, drops it back into Edith's purse.

The New Myth

Lise walks through the auditorium doors past
the back seats, no longer a young woman hiding.
She takes a seat between friends. They face
King Gustav, who sits on a throne among potted flowers.

Otto stands to speak of the discovery of nuclear fission.
We becomes *I*. He accepts an award
for experiments she designed and whose results
she explained, saying the atom's nucleus split
and released energy. She, not he, realized
the atomic numbers of krypton and barium
added together to make that of uranium.
She alone calculated the enormous energy
the splitting would release.

The hall seems darker. Sitting on either side of Lise,
Niels and Hilde stiffen their necks as Otto talks
about the discovery but doesn't say Lise's name.
She hears her friends' heavy, angry breath
and prepares to say to them later:
It's only a gold medal. We know the truth.
Still, she is glad when Hilde holds her cold hand.

Once Lise and her work were hidden for safety.
Fear taught Otto to duck. The war is over,

but hiding has become habit. He created
a story he thinks works fine without her name.
Maybe it works better. Everyone likes
the myth of a brilliant man working alone.

A Table for Two

The next day Lise opens newspapers that describe
her as a former *Mitarbeiterin*: an assistant.
As if she hadn't headed the physics department
next to Otto's chemistry department for twenty-one years.
Lise meets with Otto at a quiet table in a hotel lobby.
She congratulates him on the prize, then asks,
How could you speak as if I were never part of this?

I split the atoms. In Germany while you were in Sweden.

And I explained what you saw. We were a team.

*You won other prizes, brought back honorary degrees
from America. I saw your picture as Woman of the Year.*
Otto hammers out words one by one,
like nails pounded into boards for an ark
that will carry him safely forward, sailing just one way.
I need my work, he says. *You know Edith isn't well.
There are doctor bills. The laboratory
was bombed to rubble. My son lost an arm.*
He pushes an envelope toward her.
I wanted to give you some of the prize money.

She opens the envelope, quickly counts

a goodly amount, then calculates
it's ten percent of the prize. A *Trinkgeld*, a tip.
She sets it down, clenches her hands.

I wish no one used our findings
to make a bomb, Otto says.

We agree on that. She loosens her hands
slightly, then tightens them again.
Leaders in England and America were afraid
a bomb was being built in Germany.

The Nazis did many terrible things, but not that.

Lise doesn't believe this is the whole story,
but she looks down at the table.
At least today she won't ask, *How do you know*
who was or wasn't working on a bomb?

Will you come back to Berlin? Otto asks.

I don't know. She picks up the envelope,
which is much lighter than a gold medal.
Money was never her pursuit,
but she'll take the gift, which will be useful
if she returns to Berlin to see some old friends.

Lise feels hurt and betrayed by Otto.
But he helped her leave Germany, risking
his own life by aiding someone who broke Nazi laws.
During the best years of her life they worked
side by side, singing duets in the laboratory.
She won't forget the mighty team they were.

Gray, White, and Blue

LONDON, ENGLAND, 1947

Elisabeth writes that she'll be in London
to work in a research library, updating
her book about the origins of plants.
In her letters she gives only good news.
As if pulling a limp ribbon into a bow,
she twists Lise's replies into crisp cheer.
Lise misses her but won't leave Sweden for England
until Otto will be in London too, for a conference.
A third person could give truth a better chance.

They all meet in a restaurant. Elisabeth is still beautiful,
though her white hair doesn't smell like leaves.
A spray of violets is pinned under her collar,
held within a tiny silver vessel
that must keep the stems moist.
She speaks of her work adding hundreds
of newly discovered species to her book.
Going back in time can change the future.

It's been nine years since I've seen you,
Lise says. *Can we speak of that past?*

Did Elisabeth tell you she hid two women during the war?
Otto asks. *Edith helped get food to them and others.*

Andrea and her sister stayed in the garden shed,
Elisabeth says. *When that got too dangerous,*
Fritz and Maria took in Andrea.

Lise takes a breath. She remembers the seven-layer cake
Andrea baked. She supposes the rake was moved,
the damp notebooks that swelled and waved,
the photo of two young women by the river,
their straw hats strewn beside their bare feet.
Did Elisabeth hide suppers in flowerpots,
bring in news along with a spade to mislead neighbors?
Thank you, Lise says. *That was brave.*
You could have been arrested. Murdered.

I was scared. Elisabeth looks across the table,
then, quickly as turning a doorknob, down.
But we don't expect to be thanked.
It was what needed to be done. And now it's over.
We must look ahead, not back.

What use is the past if we don't let it teach us?

There were many wrongs. But we're tired, Lise.
You don't know what it was like to live in a city

under attack. In a war I hoped we'd lose.

We're working to replace the laboratories
that were bombed. Otto's thick eyebrows
are gray now. His eyes, of course, still blue.
People cut down trees in the park for firewood.
They dug out the roses to plant vegetable patches.

Lise read that Berlin is now a city of broken buildings,
shattered windows, crushed roofs, rubble, rats.
I understand help is needed to rebuild,
but someone must look at all the broken glass.

I never joined the Nazi Party, Otto says,
though that would have made my job more secure.
And you know Elisabeth was dismissed
for being honest, her teaching credentials taken.

And now can you teach again, Elisabeth?
As she speaks the name of her old friend,
Lise finds something that was lost.
She was wrong. Her hair does smell like leaves.

Yes. Elisabeth can't repress a smile.
I'm now a professor with tenure.

That last word rings like tossed tin.

A woman like Elisabeth is welcomed back
to the university, while no one apologized
to Lise for dismissing her.
No one asked her to come back.
She manages to murmur, *Congratulations.*

Did Edith write to you that Hanno and his wife
had a baby boy? Otto asks. *You should come visit.*

I sent my good wishes to Hanno
and his family. How are they?

Hungry. Everything is hard. No one wants to help.
We can't get food shipped from other countries.
The left side of Otto's mouth flickers down.
Milk and butter are hardly to be seen.
Will we always be punished for the crimes of just some?

Lise gives Otto back the gold ring
that could have saved her life. She says,
If you think it might help, I'll send Hanno
and his wife powdered milk for the baby.

White as Snow

The new German government asks Lise
and many Jewish survivors for testimonials
of the character of co-workers who joined the Nazi Party.
They want to know who performed horrors
and who didn't start crimes, but didn't try to stop them.
People call the forms *Persilscheine* after the soap powder
with the slogan: *To wash white as snow.*
Like laundry or paper, people can change.
But the past can't be washed away.

Small things matter, like not welcoming a woman
into a bakery, but Lise is asked only
about colleagues at KWI. She sits by geraniums,
a chocolate bar, and a stack of their letters.
All her former assistants declare
they weren't ever truly Nazis
but went along because they needed jobs.
One pleads: *I have three children to feed
and can't go to prison.* Another apologizes
for not writing to her for all these years:
*I wasn't anti-Semitic, but a young man
finds it hard to take directions from a woman.*
Everyone claims: *I knew nothing about deaths.*

Lise chooses her words carefully:
I never heard him speak propaganda.
She receives a questionnaire about Kurt Hess.
Was he a Nazi? she is asked. *Yes, of course.*
Did he attack you in particular?
She remembers him listening by her door.

Lise won't be like the Lord, who cast
a line between the worthy and the wicked.
She won't be like Noah, who called
some people to safety and left others behind.
If she must choose who she'd be,
she'd be the rising water, a flood of grief
and fury for people who were told
they weren't good enough and deserted.
Surely someone aboard the ark wished they had tried
to fit in another duck or two, another tiger.
Before they set sail, everyone should have stood
together in the rain, held hands by the rising water.

Lise looks at the questionnaire that draws straight lines
between right and wrong, which doesn't match life
as she knew it in Berlin. Naming those most at fault
may only give an excuse for others to claim innocence.
Kurt Hess was corrupt, but so were many.
Lise drops the paper with his name into the wastebasket.
She wants to find ways to hold forgiveness and truth.

Old Friend

Fritz telephones. He tells Lise that Otto also offered
him money from the Nobel Prize. *Maria and I*
won't take anything from a man who didn't stand
to say you were the intellectual leader of our team
from start to finish. But that's not why I called.
I head the physics department now,
which at the moment means overseeing repairs
of what used to be KWI. It will have a new name.
Germany is done with emperors
with shiny helmets and swords.
It's now the Max Planck Institute.
We hope you'll come here to do research.

Lise remembers Fritz saying he'd earn a living
cutting stone before he'd go against his conscience.
She's glad that honorable people like him
who once were banned from the university
are now promoted. She's moved by the offer
from someone she would never doubt.
But she wouldn't be working with Fritz alone.
Banners with swastikas are gone from Berlin,
but nail holes remain.

There can be no science without trust.

Lise taps the envelope with the money Otto gave her.
She'll send it to the group Einstein
helped found to build world peace.
She says, *I miss you, Fritz. But I won't return.*

A New Home

In retirement from her professorship in Sweden,
Lise walks through meadows shaded by grand oaks
near Cambridge University, where Robert teaches.
He married an artist Lise loves.
They're raising two good children.
Now in her eighties, Lise's steps are smaller,
her voice crinkled and low. She's often cold.

Tonight she sits by the hearth amid boxes packed
with letters, her address book with crossed-off names,
notebooks with records of scientific studies.
Not everything is here, but a glimpse of strawberries,
snapdragons, certificates, medals, lace collars,
the uneven, meticulous path to discovering
nuclear fission before a word existed for such.
She'll ask Robert to bring the cartons
to the college archives. Someday, someone might find
paper trails of her faithfulness to work and friends.
Perhaps they'll see how deeply she loved
the visible and invisible world.

The Edge of the Woods

CAMBRIDGE, ENGLAND, 1968

Robert kneels on the moss by the gravestone
he chose, engraved with the words:
A PHYSICIST WHO NEVER LOST HER HUMANITY.
Morning light slants on red and blue flowers
across the cemetery near the trees.
Are they snapdragons? Robert is not good
with the names of plants
but remembers these as his aunt's favorite.

Robert's arms are sore from carrying cartons
of scientific diagrams and diaries to the library.
He looked through some letters:
Dear Otto, Dear Edith, Dear Elisabeth—
was that the woman who was smitten with plants?
He found an old copy of a periodic table
with elements added in her handwriting
and a small wooden duck. He vaguely recalls a toy ark.
Like light, stories wave and swell more than end.

He walks toward the birch and oak trees,
sees that what he thought were flowers are shrubs.
He doesn't believe Lise was religious,

but faith is as mysterious as science.

Maybe she'd want a prayer. *Remember her.*

He picks up a stone and whispers, *Remember.*

A Note from the Author

After World War II, Lise Meitner (1878–1968) did research at Sweden's Royal Institute of Technology. When she retired at age seventy-five, she moved to England to be near her favorite nephew and his family. She arranged to leave her scientific notes, diaries, and letters to the Cambridge University archives. As years passed, admiration of her remained strong in scientific communities, but some of her accomplishments were hidden beneath tributes to Otto Hahn, her thirty-year scientific partner. Writers, particularly Lise Meitner's biographers, Ruth Lewin Sime and Patricia Rife, helped direct a light back on her extraordinary life. Her name is now on buildings, including the Lise-Meitner-Haus Department of Physics at Humboldt University, the former University of Berlin. Craters on the moon and on Venus were named after her. A highly radioactive element was named meitnerium.

Hidden Powers: Lise Meitner's Call to Science is a work of imagination and historical interpretation. I owe a great debt to the intrepid biographers of Lise Meitner and her colleagues, writers about science, politics, and the culture of twentieth-century Europe. I used verse to compress Lise Meitner's life, while drawing small recorded moments, or long habits of work, into scenes. I strived to stay true to family events, discoveries, and career advancements that are part of the public record, and I used these historical events as a frame. Composing with details common to the time and place, I blended facts with empathy to deepen a sense of how events may have felt and to show the truth that a scientist is more than a scientist. I leaned on bits of recorded conversations, but more often created dialogue based on what I learned about people's beliefs. My hope throughout was to honor a brilliant and courageous woman of science.

Timeline

NOVEMBER 7, 1878 Lise Meitner is born in Vienna, Austria.

MARCH 8, 1879 Otto Hahn is born in Frankfurt, Germany.

MARCH 14, 1879 Albert Einstein is born in Ulm, Germany.

1901 Lise Meitner starts classes at the University of Vienna, which opened to women in 1900.

1906 Lise Meitner receives a PhD in physics from the University of Vienna.

1907 Lise Meitner moves to Berlin, Germany, and begins work at the University of Berlin, where she forges a thirty-year partnership with Otto Hahn.

1912 Lise Meitner is the first woman at the University of Berlin to be hired as an assistant, working with Max Planck.

1913 Emil Fischer offers Lise Meitner a salary to work at the Kaiser Wilhelm Institute in the Hahn-Meitner Laboratory.

1914 World War I begins.

JULY 1915–OCTOBER 1916 Lise Meitner works as an X-ray technician and nurse in the Austrian army.

1918 Lise Meitner and Otto Hahn announce the discovery of protactinium, element 91, after Otto Hahn returns from the war.

1922 Lise Meitner, who has now published about forty scientific papers, becomes a full professor in the physics department at the University of Berlin.

1924 Richard Willstätter resigns from the University of Munich to protest anti-Semitism.

JANUARY 30, 1933 Adolf Hitler is appointed chancellor of Germany.

APRIL 7, 1933 Hitler has been in power for ten weeks when the Law for the Restoration of the Professional Civil Service is passed, declaring that people of non-Aryan descent or anyone opposed to Nazi principles may be dismissed from government-funded jobs. Lise Meitner and thousands of other educators are dismissed.

MAY 10, 1933 In Berlin and other cities throughout Germany, over forty thousand books are burned.

SEPTEMBER 1935 Germany passes the Nuremberg Laws, which state that Jewish people are not German citizens. They lose many of their rights.

MARCH 1938 In what's known as the Anschluss, German troops march into Austria, which becomes part of Germany and subject to its racial laws.

JULY 1938 Lise escapes from Germany to the Netherlands, then settles in Sweden.

NOVEMBER 9, 1938 On Kristallnacht, or "The Night of Broken Glass," in Germany and Austria, Jewish shops and homes are vandalized, thousands of synagogues are set on fire, and about thirty thousand Jewish men are arrested.

DECEMBER 1938 Enrico Fermi wins the Nobel Prize. Shortly afterward, with the help of Niels Bohr, he and his family furtively leave for the United States.

DECEMBER 24, 1938 While considering experiments she did with Otto Hahn and Fritz Strassmann, Lise Meitner discovers nuclear fission.

SEPTEMBER 1939 Great Britain and France declare war against Germany. World War II begins.

MAY 1945 Germany surrenders to the Allies.

AUGUST 6, 1945 In Hiroshima, Japan, more than seventy thousand people die in an atomic explosion that's thousands of times hotter than the sun. Three days later another bomb is dropped on the Japanese city of Nagasaki.

JANUARY 1946 Lise Meitner is named Woman of the Year by the Women's National Press Club in New York City.

DECEMBER 1946 Otto Hahn receives a Nobel Prize in Chemistry "for his discovery of the fission of heavy nuclei."

1953 At age seventy-five, Lise retires from the Royal Institute of Technology in Stockholm, Sweden, where her research supported ways to use nuclear fission to make heat and light, run machines, and advance medicine.

1966 Lise Meitner, Otto Hahn, and Fritz Strassmann jointly win an award named after Enrico Fermi, who died in 1954. This is the first time a woman wins one of most prestigious honors in science.

OCTOBER 27, 1968 Lise Meitner dies in England a few days before she would turn ninety.

1997 Meitnerium, element 109, is named as a tribute to Lise Meitner.

Friends and Colleagues

Most of the people important to Lise Meitner were scientists and public figures. The real people who take part in this verse narrative are listed below, set loosely in order of when they entered Lise's life.

(OTTO) ROBERT FRISCH (1904–1979) was Lise's beloved nephew. He worked as a physicist in Germany, Denmark, and England before joining researchers in Los Alamos, New Mexico. (He was called Robert within his family, but in America took up "Otto" to distinguish himself from other scientists named Robert.) After the war he returned to England, married Ulla Blau, a graphic artist, had two children, and taught at Cambridge University for about thirty years. Lise joined his family in England after she retired.

MAX PLANCK (1858–1947) taught and directed science programs at the University of Berlin for many years. He won a Nobel Prize in Physics in 1918 for his discovery of energy quanta. Shortly before his death, the Kaiser Wilhelm Institute was renamed the Max Planck Institute for the Advancement of Science.

OTTO HAHN (1879–1968) was a highly esteemed chemist in Germany through most of his life. Most information about **EDITH HAHN (1887–1968)** is from her husband's memoir, which notes that she stopped painting after their wedding and suffered episodes of mental illness that meant she spent time in sanatoriums. Their son **HANNO HAHN (1922-1960)** served in the Nazi armed forces. After the war, he married, had one child, and became an art historian. He and his wife died in a car accident.

RICHARD WILLSTÄTTER (1872-1942) won a Nobel Prize in Chemistry in 1915 for his studies of plant pigments. He researched and taught at the University of Berlin, KWI, and the University of Munich, a position he resigned from in 1924 to protest anti-Semitism.

JAMES FRANCK (1882-1964) won a Nobel Prize in Physics in 1925, shared with Gustav Ludwig Hertz, for their studies of electrons. After leaving Germany in 1933, then Denmark the following year, James Franck taught at the University of Chicago. During World War II, he became part of a group there working on developing an atomic bomb. In 1945 he drafted a letter signed by dozens of his scientific colleagues advocating that the bomb not be dropped on cities, or at the least not without advance warning. This letter sent to politicians and military leaders was not heeded.

MAX VON LAUE (1879-1960) was awarded a Nobel Prize in 1914 for his X-ray studies. He protested Nazi policies while staying in Germany to continue his scientific work and remained a friend and correspondent of Lise after she left the country. His daughter Hildy was among the young women Lise mentored. She worked at KWI during the war and through her letters kept Lise informed of who seemed trustworthy there.

ELISABETH SCHIEMANN (1881-1972) began studying at the University of Berlin when it opened to women and received her PhD on fungi mutations in 1912. In 1922 she began work as an unpaid assistant professor. In 1940 she was dismissed and her right to teach revoked for what was called "political unreliability." Her resistance work included hiding, along with her sister Gertrud, Andrea and Valerie Wolffenstein, who were in danger of being taken to a concentration camp. Both women survived the war in hiding. In 1946, Elisabeth was made a tenured professor at the University of Berlin. She was a founder of archaeobotany, the study of the relationship of people and plants through history.

EVA VON BAHR-BERGIUS (1874-1962) received a PhD in 1908 for her work on infrared radiation and became the first woman to teach physics in a Swedish university. From 1909 to 1914 in Berlin, she published eight articles on heat radiation in gases. She returned to Sweden shortly after World War I began and taught science in a trade school. Eva helped arrange Lise Meitner's escape to Sweden and was active in other resistance work during World War II.

MARIE SKLODOWSKA CURIE (1867-1934) won a Nobel Prize in Physics for the discovery of radioactivity, a term she coined. This 1903 prize was shared with her husband **PIERRE CURIE**

(1859–1906) and **HENRI BECQUEREL** (1852–1908), men Lise admired but knew only through their work. Shortly after Pierre Curie died after being struck by a horse and carriage, Marie took over his job as a professor at the University of Paris. She was the first woman to teach there. Pierre's father helped raise the Curie daughters while Marie continued her research. In 1911 she became the first person to win a second Nobel Prize, for the discovery of radium.

IRÈNE CURIE (1897–1956) worked with her mother in the Radium Institute Marie Curie founded. As her parents did, Irène married a trusted colleague. When Irène and **FRÉDÉRIC JOLIOT-CURIE** (1900–1958) were awarded a Nobel Prize for their discovery of artificial radioactivity in 1935, Irène became the second woman to win a Nobel Prize in science. Both Irène and Frédéric risked their lives in the resistance against the Nazi occupation of France and died relatively young from illnesses caused by exposure to radioactivity.

ALBERT EINSTEIN (1879–1955) is probably the most famous scientist of the twentieth century, known for his theories on mass and energy and relativity. He won the Nobel Prize in Physics in 1921. Some historians believe that his first wife, physicist Mileva Marić-Einstein (1875–1948), helped shape some of her husband's theories, and she certainly worked on the math behind them. Most of her scientific work stopped while she devoted herself to raising their two sons in Switzerland.

NIELS BOHR (1885–1962) won the Nobel Prize in Physics in 1922 for his groundbreaking theories on the structure of the atom. He and other Danish and Swedish resisters and fishermen helped save the lives of about eight thousand Jewish-Danish citizens at risk of being captured and taken to concentration camps.

MAX DELBRÜCK (1906–1981) was dismissed from the University of Berlin for refusing to join the Nazi Party. He moved to the United States, where he used atomic theory to show the stability of genes.

LEO SZILARD (1898–1964) was born in Hungary but did much of his physics research in Germany. Shortly after Hitler gained power, he fled to England and helped found an organization to help refugee scholars find new jobs. In 1938 he moved to the United States, where he developed important theories of nuclear chain reactions and worked in Chicago to create a nuclear reactor.

HERTHA SPONER (1895–1968) was dismissed from her university job after Hitler came to power and women were removed from positions of authority. She became the first woman to teach in the physics department at Duke University. She was hired despite the administration receiving a letter from Robert Millikan, the president of the California Institute of Technology, advising that a woman on the faculty would damage the university's reputation. (Caltech did not hire a woman professor until 1969.) Hertha Sponer taught at Duke University from 1936 to 1966.

HEDWIG KOHN (1887-1964) was dismissed from her job at Breslau University, now the University of Wrocław, in 1933 for being Jewish. Lise and others helped her escape to Sweden, then to the United States. She taught at Wellesley College from 1942 to 1952.

DIRK COSTER (1889-1950) discovered the element hafnium working with George de Hevesy. Coster became a professor at the University of Groningen. He and his wife, Miep, helped Lise escape from Germany and were part of the resistance movement in Holland during World War II.

GEORGE DE HEVESY (1885-1966) and **HILDE LEVI** (1909-2003) worked in Copenhagen, Denmark, where they published papers on radiochemistry from 1934 to 1940. After they and others escaped to Sweden in the fall of 1943, Hilde worked on photosynthesis and radiocarbon dating. When Hilde retired, she returned to Copenhagen to help organize the Niels Bohr archives.

ENRICO FERMI (1901-1954) was famous in Rome, Italy, for his research on radioactive elements. After emigrating to the United States, he oversaw the first nuclear reaction in Chicago in December 1942. The Fermi family remained in the United States after World War II. His wife, **LAURA FERMI** (1907-1977), became a writer, with work often focusing on the lives of scientists. Her father was murdered at the Auschwitz concentration camp.

PAUL ROSBAUD (1896–1963) studied X-rays and metals before editing scientific books and magazines. After the founder of the important magazine *Naturwissenschaften,* or *The Science of Nature,* was dismissed for being Jewish in 1933, Paul took over that work. He knew many scientists around Europe, which helped him move between countries and work as a spy for the Allies. His wife, **HILDEGARD FRANK ROSBAUD** (1901–1997), supported that work in England. Their daughter, Angelika Rosbaud, joined the Auxiliary Territorial Service, the women's branch of the British Army founded in 1938.

FRANK FOLEY (1884–1958) was a spy for England while working at the British Passport Control Office in Berlin and later in Sweden and Norway. Acting on his Catholic faith, he helped thousands of Jewish people escape the Nazis. Frank Foley, Elisabeth Schiemann, and Fritz Strassmann were named Righteous Among the Nations, non-Jews who risked their lives to save Jewish people during the Holocaust. Along with many other people of strong conscience, they are memorialized by a grove of trees in Israel.

Selected Bibliography

Conkling, Winifred. *Radioactive! How Irène Curie and Lise Meitner Revolutionized Science and Changed the World.* Chapel Hill, NC: Algonquin Young Readers, 2016.

Hakim, Joy. *The Story of Science: Einstein Adds a New Dimension.* Washington, DC: Smithsonian Books, 2007.

McGrayne, Sharon Bertsch. *Nobel Prize Women in Science: Their Lives, Struggles, and Momentous Discoveries.* New York: Birch Lane Press, 1993.

Nelson, Craig. *The Age of Radiance: The Epic Rise and Dramatic Fall of the Atomic Era.* New York: Scribner, 2014.

Rhodes, Richard. *The Making of the Atomic Bomb: The 25th Anniversary Edition.* New York: Simon & Schuster, 2012.

Rife, Patricia. *Lise Meitner and the Dawn of the Nuclear Age.* Boston: Birkhäuser, 1999.

Sime, Ruth Lewin. *Lise Meitner: A Life in Physics.* Berkeley: University of California Press, 1996.

JEANNINE ATKINS is the author of several critically acclaimed books for young readers about courageous women, including *Grasping Mysteries: Girls Who Loved Math*; *Finding Wonders: Three Girls Who Changed Science*; *Stone Mirrors: The Sculpture and Silence of Edmonia Lewis*; and *Borrowed Names: Poems About Laura Ingalls Wilder, Madam C. J. Walker, Marie Curie, and Their Daughters*. Jeannine teaches writing for children and young adults at Simmons University. She lives in western Massachusetts. Visit her at jeannineatkins.com.